LOSING IT

LOSING IT

CORA CARMACK

EBURY
PRESS

3 5 7 9 10 8 6 4 2

First published in the United States of America in 2012 by William Morrow
Paperbacks, an imprint of HarperCollins Publishers
Published in the UK in 2013 by Ebury Press, an imprint of Ebury Publishing
A Random House Group Company

The Random House Group Limited Reg. No. 954009

Addresses for companies within the Random House Group can be found at:
www.randomhouse.co.uk

A CIP catalogue record for this book is available from the British Library

The Random House Group Limited supports the Forest Stewardship Council®
(FSC®), the leading international forest-certification organisation. Our books
carrying the FSC label are printed on FSC®-certified paper. FSC is the only
forest-certification scheme supported by the leading environmental organisations,
including Greenpeace. Our paper procurement policy can be found at
www.randomhouse.co.uk/environment

Printed and bound by CPI Group (UK) Ltd, Croydon, CR0 4YY

ISBN 9780091953386

To buy books by your favourite authors and register for offers visit:
www.randomhouse.co.uk

For Lindsay

My first reader.
Thank you for all the times you've listened to me vent.
You've heard every mortifying story.
You've been there through the awkward, the hilarious,
and the near-death experiences.
Stone love.

took a deep breath.

You are awesome. I didn't quite believe it, so I thought it again.

Awesome. You are so awesome. If my mother heard my thoughts, she'd tell me that I needed to be humble, but humility had gotten me nowhere.

Bliss Edwards, you are a freaking catch.

So then how did I end up twenty-two years old and the only person I knew who had never had sex? Somewhere between *Saved by the Bell* and *Gossip Girl,* it became unheard of for a girl to graduate college with her V-card still in hand. And now I was standing in my room, regretting that I'd gathered the courage to admit it to my friend Kelsey. She reacted like I'd just told her I was hiding a tail underneath my A-line skirt. And I knew before her jaw even finished dropping that this was a terrible idea.

"*Seriously?* Is it because of Jesus? Are you, like, saving yourself for him?" Sex seemed simpler for Kelsey. She had the body of a Barbie and the sexually charged brain of a teenage boy.

"No, Kelsey," I said. "It would be a little difficult to save myself for someone who died over two thousand years ago."

Kelsey whipped off her shirt and threw it on the floor. I must have made a face because she looked at me and laughed.

"Relax, Princess Purity, I'm just changing shirts." She stepped into my closet and started flipping through my clothes.

"Why?"

"Because, Bliss, we're going out to get you laid." She said the word "laid" with a curl of her tongue that reminded me of those late-night commercials for those adult phone lines.

"Jesus, Kelsey."

She pulled out a shirt that was snug on me and would be downright scandalous on her curvy frame.

"What? You said it wasn't about him."

I resisted the urge to slam my palm into my forehead.

"It's not, I don't think . . . I mean, I go to church and all, well, sometimes. I just . . . I don't know. I've never been that interested."

She paused with her new shirt halfway over her head.

"Never interested? In guys? Are you gay?"

I once overheard my mother, who can't understand why

I'm about to graduate college without a ring on my finger, ask my father the same question.

"No, Kelsey, I'm not gay, so keep putting your shirt on. No need to fall on your sexual sword for me."

"If you're not gay and it's not about Jesus, then it's just a matter of finding the right guy, or should I say . . . the right sexual sword."

I rolled my eyes. "Gee? Is that all? Find the right guy? Why didn't someone tell me sooner?"

She pulled her blond hair back into a high ponytail, which somehow drew even more attention to her chest. "I don't mean the right guy to marry, honey. I mean the right guy to get your blood pumping. To make you turn off your analytical, judgmental, hyperactive brain and think with your body instead."

"Bodies can't think."

"*See!*" she said. "Analytical. Judgmental."

"Fine! Fine. Which bar tonight?"

"Stumble Inn, of course."

I groaned. "Classy."

"What?" Kelsey looked at me like I was missing the answer to a really obvious question. "It's a good bar. More importantly, it's a bar that guys like. And since we *do* like guys, it's a bar *we* like."

It could be worse. She could be taking me to a club.

"Fine. Let's go." I stood and headed for the curtain that separated my bedroom from the rest of my loft apartment.

"*Whoa!* Whoa." She grabbed my elbow and pulled me so hard that I fell back on my bed. "You can't go like that."

I looked down at my outfit—a flowery A-line skirt and

simple tank that showed a decent amount of cleavage. I looked cute. I could totally pick up a guy in this . . . maybe.

"I don't see the problem," I said.

She rolled her eyes, and I felt like a child. I hated feeling like a child, and I pretty much always did when talk turned to sex.

Kelsey said, "Honey, right now you look like someone's adorable little sister. No guy wants to screw his little sister. And if he does, you don't want to be near him."

Yep, definitely felt like a child. "Point taken."

"Hmm . . . sounds like you're practicing turning off that overactive brain of yours. Good job. Now stand there and let me work my magic."

And by magic, she meant torture.

After vetoing three shirts that made me feel like a prostitute, some pants that were more like leggings, and a skirt so short it threatened to show the world my hoo-hoo in the event of a mild breeze, we settled on some tight low-rise denim capris and a lacy black tank that stood out in contrast to my pale white skin.

"Legs shaved?"

I nodded.

"Other . . . things . . . shaved?"

"As much as they are ever going to be, yes, now move on." That was where I drew the line of this conversation.

She grinned, but didn't argue. "Fine. Fine. Condoms?"

"In my purse."

"Brain?"

"Turned off. Or well . . . dialed down anyway."

"Excellent. I think we're ready."

I wasn't ready. Not at all.

There was a reason I hadn't had sex yet, and now I knew it. I was a control freak. It was why I had done so well in school my entire life. It made me a great stage manager—no one could run a theater rehearsal like I could. And when I did get up the nerve to act, I was always more prepared than any other actor in class. But sex . . . that was the opposite of control. There were emotions, and attraction, and that pesky other person that just *had* to be involved. Not my idea of fun.

"You're thinking too much," Kelsey said.

"Better than not thinking enough."

"Not tonight it's not," she said.

I turned up the volume of Kelsey's iPod as soon as we got in the car so that I could think in peace.

I could do this. It was just a problem that needed to be solved, an item that needed to be checked off my to-do list.

It was that simple.

Simple.

Keep it simple.

We pulled up outside the bar several minutes later, and the night felt anything but simple. My pants felt too tight, my shirt too low-cut, and my brain too clouded. I wanted to throw up.

I didn't want to be a virgin. That much I knew. I didn't want to feel like the immature prude who knew nothing about sex. I hated not knowing things. The trouble was . . . as much as I didn't want to be a virgin, I also didn't want to have sex.

The conundrum of all conundrums. Why couldn't this be one of those square-is-a-rectangle-but-rectangle-is-not-always-a-square kind of things?

Kelsey was standing outside my door, her high-heeled shoes snapping in time with her fingers as she roused me out of the car. I squared my shoulders, tossed my hair (half-heartedly), and followed Kelsey into the bar.

I made a beeline straight to the bar, wiggled myself onto a stool, and waved down the bartender.

He was a possibility. Blond hair, average build, nice face. Nothing special, but certainly not out of the question. He could be good for simple.

"What can I get for y'all, ladies?"

Southern accent. Definitely a homegrown kind of boy.

Kelsey butted in, "We need two shots of tequila to start."

"Make it four," I croaked.

He whistled, and his eyes met mine. "That kinda night, huh?"

I wasn't ready to put into words what kind of night this was. So I just said, "I'm looking for some liquid courage."

"And I'd be glad to help." He winked at me, and he was barely out of earshot before Kelsey bounced in her seat, saying, "He's the one! He's the one!"

Her words made me feel like I was on a roller coaster, like the world had just dropped and all my organs were playing catch-up. I just needed more time to adjust. That's it. I grabbed Kelsey's shoulder and forced her to stay still. "Chill, Kels. You're like a freaking Chihuahua."

"What? He's a good choice. Cute. Nice. And I totally saw him glance at your cleavage . . . *twice.*"

She wasn't wrong. But I still wasn't all that interested in sleeping with him, which I suppose didn't have to rule him out, but this sure would be a hell of a lot easier if I was actually *interested* in the guy. I said, "I'm not sure . . . there's just no spark." I could see an eye roll coming, so I tagged on a quick "Yet!"

When Bartender Boy returned with our drinks, Kelsey paid and I took my two shots before she even handed over her card. He stayed for a moment, smiling at me, before moving on to another customer. I stole one of Kelsey's remaining shots.

"You're lucky this is a big night for you, Bliss. Normally, nobody gets between me and my tequila."

I held my hand out and said, "Well, nobody will get between these legs unless I'm good and drunk, so hand me the last one."

Kelsey shook her head, but she was smiling. After a few seconds, she gave in, and with four shots of tequila in my system the prospect of sex seemed a little less scary.

Another bartender came by, this one a girl, and I ordered a Jack and Coke to sip on while I puzzled through this whole mess.

There was Bartender Boy, but he wouldn't get off until well after 2:00 A.M. I was a nervous wreck already, so if this dragged on till the wee hours of the morning, I'd be completely psychotic. I could just imagine it . . . straitjacketed due to sex.

There was a guy standing next to me who seemed to move several inches closer with every drink I took, but he had to be at least forty. No thank you.

I gulped down more of my drink, thankful the bartender had gone heavy on the Jack, and scanned the bar.

"What about him?" Kelsey asked, pointing to a guy at a nearby table.

"Too preppy."

"Him?"

"Too hipster."

"Over there?"

"Ew. Too hairy."

The list continued until I was pretty sure this night was a bust. Kelsey suggested we hit another bar, which was the last thing I wanted to do. I told her I had to go to the bathroom, hoping someone would catch her eye while I was gone so that I could slip away with no drama. The bathroom was at the back, past the pool and darts area, behind a section with some small round tables.

That was when I noticed him.

Well, technically, I noticed the book first.

And I just couldn't keep my mouth closed. "If that's supposed to be a way to pick up girls, I would suggest moving to an area with a little more traffic."

He looked up from his reading, and suddenly I found it hard to swallow. He was easily the most attractive guy I'd seen tonight—blond hair falling into crystal blue eyes, just enough scruff on his jaw to give him a masculine look without making him too hairy, and a face that could have made angels sing. It wasn't making me sing. It was making me gawk. Why did I stop? Why did I always have to make an idiot of myself?

"Excuse me?"

My mind was still processing his perfect hair and bright blue eyes, so it took me a second to say, "Shakespeare. No one reads Shakespeare in a bar unless it's a ploy to pick up girls. All I'm saying is, you might have better luck up front."

He didn't say anything for a long beat, but then his mouth split in a grin revealing, what do you know, perfect teeth!

"It's not a ploy, but if it were, it seems to me that I'm having great luck right here."

An accent. *He has a British accent.* Dear God, I'm dying.

Breathe. I needed to breathe.

Don't lose it, Bliss.

He put his book down, but not before marking his place. My God, he was really reading Shakespeare in a bar.

"You're not trying to pick up a girl?"

"I wasn't."

My analytical brain did not miss his use of the past tense. As in . . . he hadn't been trying to seduce anyone before, but perhaps he was now.

I took another look at him. He was grinning now—white teeth, jaw stubble that made him look downright delectable. Yep, I was definitely seducible. And that thought alone was enough to send me into shock.

"What's your name, beautiful?"

Beautiful? *Beautiful!* Still dying here.

"Bliss."

"Is that a line?"

I blushed crimson. "No, it's my name."

"Lovely name for a lovely girl." The timbre of his voice went into that low register that made my insides curl in on themselves—it was like my uterus was tapping out a happy dance on the rest of my organs. God, I was dying the longest, most torturous, most arousing death in the history of the world. Was this what it always felt like to be turned on? No wonder sex made people do crazy things.

"Well, Bliss, I'm new in town, and I've already locked myself out of my apartment. I'm waiting on a locksmith actually, and I figured I'd put this spare time to good use."

"By brushing up on your Shakespeare?"

"Trying to anyway. Honestly, I've never liked the bloke all that much, but let's keep that a secret between us, yeah?"

I'm pretty sure my cheeks were still stained red, if the heat coming off of them was any indication. In fact, my whole body felt like it was on fire. I'm not sure whether it was mortification or his accent that had me about to spontaneously combust in front of him.

"You look disappointed, Bliss. Are you a Shakespeare fan?"

I nodded, because my throat might have been closing up.

He wrinkled his nose in response, and my hands itched to follow the line of his nose down to his lips.

I was going crazy. Actually, certifiably insane.

"Don't tell me you're a *Romeo and Juliet* fan?"

Now this. *This* was something I could discuss.

"*Othello* actually. That's my favorite."

"Ah. Fair Desdemona. Loyal and pure."

My heart stuttered at the word "pure."

"I, um . . ." I struggled to piece together my thoughts. "I like the juxtaposition of reason and passion."

"I'm a fan of passion myself." His eyes dipped down then and ran the length of my form. My spine tingled until it felt like it might burst out of my skin.

"You haven't asked me my name," he said.

I cleared my throat. This couldn't be attractive. I was about as sociable as a caveman. I asked, "What's your name?"

He tilted his head, and his hair almost covered his eyes.

"Join me, and I'll tell you."

I didn't think about anything other than the fact that my legs were like Jell-O and sitting down would prevent me from doing something embarrassing, like passing out from the influx of hormones that were quite clearly having a free-for-all in my brain. I sank into the chair, but instead of feeling relieved, the tension ratcheted up another notch.

He spoke, and my eyes snagged on his lips. "My name is Garrick."

Who knew names could be hot too?

"It's nice to meet you, Garrick."

He leaned forward on his elbows, and I noticed his broad shoulders and the way his muscles moved beneath the fabric of his shirt. Then our eyes connected, and the bar around us went from dim to dark, while I was ensnared by those baby blues.

"I'm going to buy you a drink." It wasn't meant to be a question. In fact, when he looked at me, there was nothing questioning in him at all, only confidence. "Then we can chat some more about reason and . . . passion."

2

I couldn't tell whether the burning sensation in my chest had to do with the hooded look Garrick was giving me or the remainder of my first Jack and Coke that I had just downed like it was water.

A waiter arrived at Garrick's beckoning, and I took a moment to give myself a silent pep talk while he ordered himself a drink.

"Bliss?" Garrick prompted.

His voice sent shivers through me.

I looked up at him, then at the waiter, who happened to be Bartender Boy from earlier. I opened my mouth to ask for another Jack and Coke, but Bartender Boy stopped me with a hand on my shoulder. "I remember—Jack and Coke, right?"

I nodded, and he threw me a wink and a smile. I paused, wondering for a second how he knew my order. I was pretty sure the girl bartender had served me last. He was still smiling at me, so I forced myself to speak. "Thanks, um . . ."

"Brandon," he supplied.

"Thanks, Brandon."

He glanced at Garrick, and then focused back on me.

"Should I tell your friend up front that you'll be right back?"

"Oh, um, sure, I guess."

He smiled in response and stayed there staring at me for a few seconds before he turned to head back to the bar. I knew I had to look at Garrick again, but I was terrified I'd melt into a puddle of arousal and awkwardness if I met his gorgeous eyes again.

He said, "You know, sometimes I wonder if Desdemona was as innocent as she let on. Maybe she knew the effect she had on guys and enjoyed making them jealous."

I met his eyes then, and they were narrowed, studying me.

I swallowed my nerves and studied him back.

"Or maybe she was just intimidated by Othello's intensity and didn't know how to talk to him. Communication is key, after all."

"Communication, eh?"

"It could have solved a lot of their problems."

"In that case, I'll endeavor to be as clear as possible." He picked up his chair and placed it mere inches from mine. He slinked down beside me and said, "I'd rather you didn't go back to your friend. Stay here with me."

Swallow, Bliss. I told myself. *You have to swallow or you might start drooling.*

"Well, my friend is waiting. What will we do if I stay?"

He reached out a hand and pushed my hair over my shoulder. His hand skimmed across my neck, pausing at my pulse point, which must have been going crazy.

"We can talk Shakespeare. We can talk about anything you want. Though I can't promise not to get distracted by your lovely neck." His fingers traveled across my jaw, until they reached my chin, which he pulled forward slightly with the pressure of his index finger. "Or your lips. Or those eyes. I could woo you with stories about my life, like Othello does Desdemona."

I was already sufficiently wooed. My reply was embarrassingly breathy. "I'd rather not parallel our evening with a couple who ended with a murder-suicide."

He grinned, and his finger dropped from my chin. My skin burned where he had touched me, and I had to stop myself from leaning forward to follow his touch.

"Touché. I don't care what we do as long as you stay."

"Okay." I was immensely proud that I managed a calm reply instead of the *Dear God, yes, I'll do whatever you ask* that was currently running through my mind.

"Maybe I should lock myself out of my apartment more often."

I'd prefer we locked ourselves in actually.

My pocket started vibrating, and I rushed to answer my phone before my embarrassing boyband ringtone came on.

"Yes?"

"Did you fall in or what?"

It was Kelsey.

"No, Kelsey, I didn't. Listen, why don't you just head home without me?"

Garrick's eyes darkened, and my breath hitched as his gaze dropped to my lips.

"You are not getting out of this, Bliss. You are getting laid tonight if I have to do it myself."

God, could she be any louder? I thought that Garrick had to have heard, but his eyes never left my lips.

"That won't be necessary, Kels."

I tried to think of a cryptic way to tell her that I'd already found my guy, when I heard an intake of breath followed by "*Oh. My. God.*"

I glanced over Garrick's shoulder in time to see Kelsey's grin widen, and the crude hand gesture that followed.

"Yeah, okay, so I'll talk to you later, Kels?"

"You most certainly will. You'll call and tell me every drop-dead gorgeous detail."

"We'll see."

"You better do a lot of seeing tonight, honey. I expect your eyes to be fully opened after this evening's encounter."

I hung up without replying.

"Your friend?" he asked.

I nodded because his stare had my blood boiling. Never in my life had I felt so completely turned on by someone who was not even touching me. Sex rolled off the man in waves, and I was surprised to find how interested I was in learning how to swim.

"You're staying?"

I nodded again, every muscle in my body drawn taut. If

he didn't kiss me soon, I was going to explode. Just when I thought he might, Bartender Boy returned with our drinks. He came up with a smile, which dropped upon seeing how close Garrick and I were.

"Sorry it took so long. We're swamped up front."

I latched on to the distraction.

"It's no problem, Brandon."

"Sure. You need anything else?"

"No, I'm good."

Brandon's eyes flicked to Garrick, and then he leaned a little closer to me.

"You sure?"

"We're sure," Garrick tagged on curtly before handing him a few bills. "Keep the change."

Brandon checked on one more couple a few tables away, and then he left for the front of the bar again. When he was out of earshot, I turned back to Garrick. I noticed his arm had made its way around my chair.

"Are you the jealous type, Garrick?"

"Not really."

I raised an eyebrow, and he smiled unabashedly.

He said, "Maybe this discussion of Othello has set me a bit on edge."

"Then let's talk about something else. What time did the locksmith say he'd be around to your apartment?"

He glanced briefly at his watch, and I took the chance to eye the incredible build of his arms. "He should be there fairly soon."

"Should you go and wait for him?" It was hard to pin-point exactly what I wanted in that moment. I definitely liked him, and I definitely wanted him to kiss me, but I was so used to sabotaging things like this so that they never got too far. I was always searching for a back door, the way out.

"Are you trying to get rid of me?"

I took a breath. No backing out. No back doors, not this time. I bit my lip and looked at him. I hoped he couldn't read the fear thrumming beneath my confident facade. I said, "I guess *we* could go and wait for him."

He looked at my lips again. Dying . . . I was dying for him to kiss me.

"Much better."

He stood and offered me his arm. "Milady?"

"You don't want to finish our drinks?"

He took my hand and pressed his lips against the inside of my wrist. "I'm already intoxicated."

I laughed, because the line was ridiculous . . . and because I didn't want to admit that it still worked.

He grinned. "Too far? What can I say . . . the Bard gives me a flair for the dramatic."

"Let's try for some realism instead."

He said, "I think I can do that."

I'd barely processed his words before he'd pulled me up from the chair and covered my mouth with his own. His scent overwhelmed me—citrus and leather and something else that made my mouth water. I was almost too shocked to react. I was acutely aware of the fact that he was kissing me in the middle of a bar, until he nipped at my bottom lip. Then I forgot about everything but him. My whole body shuddered, and my heart dropped toward my stomach like the force of gravity had doubled. My head was swimming, but I didn't care. I opened my mouth, and immediately his tongue swept in, taking control. My hands clutched at his back, and in response, he pulled me closer. His kiss was slow and then fast, tender then punishing. We were pressed together so tightly that I could feel every plane of his body, but still I wanted to be closer. His hand slid up the back of my shirt—hot fingers pressed into my already overheated flesh. A moan escaped my mouth at the intimate contact. Immediately I regretted it, because the sound seemed to clear his head, and he pulled away.

I couldn't stop my lips from following him, but he stayed out of reach of my kiss. Instead, he groaned, ducked his head, and placed a hot kiss on my neck.

My brain was definitely dialed down. I was all body in that moment, and God, it felt good. I was only the sum of my nerve endings, which were going crazy. He exhaled heavily, and it scorched my skin. His voice was raspy when he spoke, "Sorry. Got carried away."

Those were exactly the right words. Carried away. I had never been so caught up in another person before. I'd never been so . . . out of control. It at once excited and terrified me.

His face appeared before mine, and I tried to keep my expression neutral. His hand slid out of my shirt, and I shivered, my skin mourning the loss.

He took a step back. "Right. Might be time for a little more reason, little less passion."

I laughed, but inside I was giving the middle finger to reason. It had ruled me long enough.

3

"You're kidding me, right?"

I stared at him, wondering if my control freak side could handle this.

His hand skimmed my jaw. "I promise I'll go slow."

I shook my head, and his hand dropped. "I don't think I can do this."

"Just hold on to me. I promise . . . you'll have fun."

"Garrick . . ."

"Bliss, just trust me."

I took a deep breath. I could do this. I just had to dial down my brain like Kelsey said.

"Okay, but hurry . . . before I change my mind."

His face split in a smile, and he placed a quick kiss on my temple. "Thatta girl."

Then he carefully fixed the helmet over my hair, threw a leg over his motorcycle, and offered me a hand. I pushed down my reservations and slipped my hand into his. The seat was curved so that even though I tried to sit a few inches back, I slid until my body was pressed right up against his.

His hand settled on my knee, his fingers curving until they tickled at the sensitive area at the back.

"Hold on to me."

I did as I was told . . . and nearly had an aneurysm when I could feel the ridges of his abs through his shirt. Suddenly I was uber-conscious of the little pudge that rested just above my jeans. He was going to take one look at my body and know that I wasn't good enough for him. Hell, he could probably feel that pudge against his back now and was already regretting this. Then the hand around my knee gave a quick tug, and even though I didn't think we could get any closer, we did.

I wasn't just pressed against him. I was plastered.

My pelvis was so tight against him that a dizzy spell tore through me. And at that same moment, we took off. I dug my hands into his middle, and he jumped, the whole motorcycle swerving to the side.

I screamed. Well, more like shrieked. Right in his ear.

He straightened us out, and then slowed to a stop at the stop sign.

"All right?"

My face buried against his shoulder, I managed to squeak out, "Yeah."

"Sorry, love, I'm just a wee bit ticklish is all."

"Oh." I loosened the fingers that were practically gouging into his sides. Thank God he couldn't see my face right now. Red was not a good look on me.

He took my hands and pulled so that my forearms were across his middle and my arms were wrapped completely around him.

"That's better. Let's give it another go."

This time when he took off, I didn't scream. He gained speed slowly, and I kept my cheek flat against his back with my eyes closed.

Shakespeare was stuck in my head from our earlier conversation, so I recited everything I knew to keep my mind busy. I started with Hamlet's soliloquy. Then moved on to the St. Crispin's Day speech from *Henry V.* I was finishing up Macbeth's "tomorrow and tomorrow and tomorrow" monologue when Garrick interrupted.

"You really do love the Bard."

Mortification was becoming my default emotion. Guess I wasn't reciting those in my head like I thought I was.

"Oh, I, um, just memorize really easily."

My cheek still against his back, I tried to calm my sprinting heart. Now that the motorcycle wasn't moving, my brain was free to fear that *other* thing that I had been actively *not* thinking about.

Sex.

I was going to have sex.

With a boy.

A hot boy.

A hot *British* boy.

Or maybe I was going to throw up.

What if I threw up on the hot British boy?

What if I threw up on the hot British boy *during sex?*

"Bliss?"

I jerked back, horrified and wondering if I accidentally spoke aloud again.

"Yes?"

"We can get off the bike anytime."

"Oh." I pulled my arms back so quickly that I nearly lost my balance and fell off the bike. Luckily, with only a minor squeak, I managed to stabilize myself and slowly slide off the bike.

Then my calf grazed a pipe on the side of the bike, and I was screaming again.

It was hot. So *freaking* hot. And now my skin was stinging.

"Bliss?"

I had limped several feet away from the bike by the time Garrick caught up to me. Despite my clenched fists, and the way I was biting down on my lip to hold in the pain, my eyes were tearing up.

His hands cupped my face first, and then he glanced down at my leg where a red welt was shining about an inch below the bottom of my capris.

"Oh bugger."

I kept my lips clamped shut, uncertain if I could open my mouth without crying. Garrick slipped an arm around my waist, and I threw one over his shoulder.

"Come on. Let's hope that locksmith has already arrived."

For the first time, I looked around and realized where we were.

We were in *my* apartment complex.

We lived in the same apartment complex!

I warred over whether I should say something as he steered me toward his apartment. I almost mentioned it when we walked past my own car, but then I reminded myself that this was supposed to be a one-night thing. He was one building over from me. Thank God. What if he had lived right beside me, and I had to see him every day after the no-doubt-terrible sex I was about to try to have with him?

We got to his door.

No locksmith.

The skin on my calf felt hot, like I was standing right next to an open flame.

He shot me a worried look, and then pulled out his phone.

He hit the call button twice, redialing the last number he called.

He stepped away from me to talk, and I leaned heavily against the wall beside his door. Clearly, I was not meant to have sex. This was God telling me that I was meant to be a nun. Get thee to a nunnery, and all that crap.

I was so delirious I was confusing God and Shakespeare.

Garrick came back, and even his frown was gorgeous.

"Bad news. The locksmith got held up and won't be here for another hour."

I tried not to cringe. I failed.

He knelt, and his fingers ran up my shin, stopping a few inches to the right of my burn. Thank God I'd shaved. He took a deep breath and released it slowly through his nose. He closed his eyes for a moment and then nodded.

"Right. Well, in that case, we should maybe take you to the emergency room."

"What? No!"

What would Kelsey say? I went out aiming to have sex, and instead I ended up in the emergency room. FML.

"Bliss, the burn isn't too bad, but if you don't start treating it, it's going to hurt like hell."

I tipped my head back against the wall and blew a stray hair out of my face. "I don't live far. We can just go to my place."

"Oh. Okay."

His grin eased back onto his face, and for a brief second I was too awash in other feelings to remember the pain. He continued: "We'll have to be careful putting you back on the motorcycle. Wouldn't want you to burn yourself again."

I bit down on my bottom lip. "We don't actually have to get on the bike."

He gracefully arched one eyebrow.

"When I say I don't live far, I mean that I live in the next building over."

Both eyebrows jumped up then. His surprise only lasted a second before a different expression crossed his face—one harder to pinpoint that made the butterflies in my stomach start having seizures.

"Let's go to your flat then . . . neighbor."

I felt weak in the knees, and not just because of the pain.

I swallowed, but my mouth still felt dry. He didn't put his arm around me again, but his fingers touched my back lightly and then stayed there as we walked. We arrived at my apartment in less than a minute. His hand dropped to my lower back as I rummaged for my keys, and for a second I forgot what I was searching for.

Keys. To my apartment.

Which he was about to enter.

With me.

Alone.

To have sex.

Sex.

Sex.

Sex.

My fingers felt broken as I tried and failed to insert the key into the lock. He didn't say anything. Nor did he take the keys from me—which was good, because that would have totally pissed me off. I might have been a mental, emotional, and physical wreck, but I didn't need a guy to turn a key for me. His hand stayed calmly, gently, patiently against my back until I managed to force the door open.

When I stepped forward into the dark hallway, his hand didn't follow. I looked back at him, standing on my porch, his hand now tucked casually into his pockets. His smile was crooked, endearing, and heart-stoppingly gorgeous. But he looked like he didn't plan to come inside. This was it. He had changed his mind. Because I was a complete mess. Why wouldn't he?

I took a breath, reminding myself that I was awesome. I was not insecure or shy. I was just a virgin. No big deal. And if I ever wanted to not be a virgin, I was going to have to have sex. Time to man, um . . . woman up.

"Are you waiting for an invitation?" I asked, eyeing him standing carefully outside my door. "Is this the part where you tell me you're a vampire?"

He chuckled. "No, I promise the paleness is only because I'm British."

"Then what are you waiting for? What happened to the guy who made me sit to find out his name and made it abundantly clear that he didn't want me going back to my friend?" What happened to the guy who was bold in ways I could only pretend to be?

He took one step, so that he stood in the doorframe, and leaned against the jamb. "That guy is trying to be a gentleman, because as much as he wanted you to come back to his place and as much as he wants to kiss you—you're hurt, and I'm afraid you don't actually want me here."

"You mean he's afraid."

"Hmm?"

"You were speaking in the third person, and then switched to first. . . ." And I was rambling.

"So I was." He was still smiling. What did that mean? "It was nice to meet you, Bliss."

This was the easy out if I didn't want to go through with this. If I wanted my virginity to see the light of day . . . again. He was turning away. All I had to do was let him go.

"Wait!"

He smiled a small, concealed smile and raised that one eyebrow again.

I breathed through my fear. "If *he's* trying to be a gentleman, shouldn't he stay and try to help the injured girl who knows nothing about treating motorcycle burns?"

His eyes left mine to glance at my calf, and when he looked up again, his eyes found my lips instead.

"The injured girl is right. It would be the gentlemanly thing to do."

Then he stepped inside my apartment and closed the door.

The light from the streetlamps outside disappeared, and we stood in the darkened hallway because my overhead light had been burnt out for weeks, and I still hadn't replaced it.

I could feel the heat radiating off of him as he stepped closer. His hand once again settled in the small of my back, and he whispered in the dark, "Lead the way, beautiful."

4

I stood in my bathroom in a tank top and underwear with my pants around my knees, on the verge of hyperventilating. Garrick was outside the door, and it was like he was a magnet. My heart kept trying to leap out of my chest toward him. He had told me to take off my capris and said that I'd need to keep from wearing tight clothes over the burn for a while. He had offered to help me get the capri pants off, but that made me feel like I was going to vomit again. So instead, I began wiggling them off myself, trying and failing to keep the fabric from touching the damaged skin.

I slid the material a bit lower and bit down on my lip to try to silence a groan.

"Bliss?" Garrick knocked lightly at the door. "You okay?"

"Just peachy!" I said back.

I pulled on the pants again and gasped.

"Bliss, just let me help. You're worrying me."

I closed my eyes, trying to think of a way around this. Hobbling awkwardly with my jeans around my knees, I found a skirt with an elastic waist in my hamper. I pulled it over my head and down to cover my underwear, then took a seat on the toilet.

I felt my cheeks, certain that they were probably a mortifying shade of red. Nothing I could do about it now. I said, "Okay. Come in."

The door swung open slowly, and Garrick's head peeked around the corner, followed by the rest of him. He took one look at my rumpled skirt, and the jeans bunched around my knees.

Then he laughed. Raucous laughter actually.

"This is so humiliating." How was I ever going to have sex with him now?

He pressed his lips together to stop the laughter, but amusement still danced in his eyes.

"I'm sorry. I know you're in pain. You just look so . . ."

"Ridiculous?"

"Cute."

I leveled him with a glare.

"Ridiculously cute."

His grin was intoxicating, and I couldn't help my begrudging smile.

"All right. Now that you've had your laugh, help me take off my pants," I said with the same sarcasm I'd been relying on since he entered.

Either he didn't catch the sarcasm or he just didn't care, because his eyes fixed on me in a way that I could only describe as downright predatory. Suddenly, much more than my leg was burning up.

He stared at me for a moment before dropping his eyes and clearing his throat. Kneeling beside me, he took my leg into his hands.

I had already started to pull the capris down, so the burn was currently covered. His hand hovered by the zipper, which was now around the middle of my thighs. He cleared his throat again and then slipped his hand down my pant leg.

Heart. Attack.

I was pretty sure I was having one.

Using his other hand, he pulled the jeans down as far as he could, just over my knees. He looked up at me, cleared his throat *again,* and said, "Can I borrow your hand?"

I couldn't speak, but I put my right hand forward, the palm of which was embarrassingly sweaty. He took my hand and pulled it inside my pant leg to join his own.

"Keep your hand here and pull the fabric as far away from your leg as you can. I'll do the same at the bottom, and we'll try to slip them off without touching the burn."

I nodded, my hand ten times steadier than my heart.

He slipped his hand up and out, his light touch sending shivers through me. He did as he said, pulling the fabric away from my skin at the bottom, and then together we tried to pull the pants off.

It wasn't the most successful mission. These jeans were indecently tight (thanks to Kelsey), and every once in a while the fabric bumped my skin and I cringed.

"Sorry," he apologized each time, like it was his fault. I wanted to correct him, but I just loved the way he said it so much that I let it go.

After a minute or two of slow and careful maneuvering, my jeans hit the floor.

We both laughed—the way you see people in movies laugh after they've just diffused a bomb. And when I stopped laughing, I realized that his hand was still on my leg. One hand was cupped around my ankle, and the other was brushing softly against the skin around the burn.

If he kept touching me like that, I was going to melt into a puddle right there on the floor.

"Um, thanks."

He seemed to realize then what he was doing. His eyes flicked quickly to his hands. Instead of pulling back immediately, he grinned, brushed his hand slowly down my leg, and then let go.

"No problem. Now we need to cool it off. We could run it under cool water." I pictured my leg hiked up to the sink, or us both trying to maneuver in my bathtub. My face must have given it away, because he added, "Or just a cool damp cloth will work."

I handed him a washcloth from a basket behind me, and he turned on the sink, waiting until the water was cool before wetting the cloth.

I sucked in a breath as he laid it across my burn, but the cool felt good, enough so that I relaxed for the first time since we'd come into my apartment.

"Better?"

I nodded. "Much. I'll never wear jeans that tight again."

He quirked a smile. "Now *that* would be a shame."

I was going to need a fan to keep myself cool if he kept saying things like that.

"Listen," he began. "I'm sorry about this. I never should have pushed you to get on that bike."

"It's not your fault I know nothing about motorcycles and didn't realize it would be hot."

"I can't believe you've never been on a motorcycle."

"Yeah, well, there are a lot of things I've never done."

He quirked one eyebrow. "Like what?"

"Well . . ." I swear my heartbeat sounded like *stu-pid, stu-pid, stu-pid,* as it pounded in my ears. "Um, until today I'd never met anyone who was British."

He laughed, combing his fingers unconsciously through his hair. It made *me* want to comb *my* fingers through his hair.

He said, "That's why you kissed me, isn't it? All you American girls seem to love accents."

I swallowed my smile and said, "I believe you were the one who kissed me."

He stood, and his messy blond hair fell over his forehead, framing those devilish eyes. "So I was."

He ran the cloth under the water again to keep it cool, but my body was too heated to really tell the difference when he placed it back on my skin. His other hand curled around my ankle again.

I kept my breath carefully steady and said, "Your turn."

"Hmm?"

"What's something you've never done?"

"Well, I've never chatted up a girl in a pub before tonight."

My jaw dropped. "Really?" How was that possible? He was gorgeous! Maybe all the girls just threw themselves at him before he even entered the bar, so he never had to bother with going inside.

He shrugged, and with the motion, his thumb started brushing back and forth against the top of my foot.

"I know it goes against the English stereotype, but I've never been much for getting sloshed, um, drunk, all the time."

"Me neither," I said. And I meant it, even though my head was still a bit fuzzy from all that tequila. "So what brings this nonstereotypical Brit to Texas?"

He shrugged. "I've been in the States for a while. I came here to go to school and never went back. I actually just moved back to Texas, though. Haven't been here for a few years."

"Me too. I just moved back here a few years ago."

I'd grown up in Texas when I was little, but we moved to Minnesota when I was in eighth grade. It had always been my plan to come back here for college.

He rewetted the cloth one more time, and we sat there talking. He told me about growing up in England, and how different it had been living in the States.

"The first time some bloke told me he liked my pants, I was so shocked I thought I'd left home missing a few key things."

"Pants? I don't understand."

"That's what we call underwear!"

"Oh," I laughed. "Good to know."

"When I asked a classmate for a rubber, you call them erasers, everyone laughed so hard that I was ready to board a flight straight back to London."

I tried to hold in my laughter and failed. But I figured he deserved it after laughing at my pants, um, jeans ordeal earlier.

"That must have been terrible."

He reached for the gauze I'd pulled down from the cabinet earlier, carefully placed it over the burn, and taped down the edges as he spoke.

"You get used to it. I've been here so long now that I usually manage well enough. Occasionally when I visit London, and come back, I have some trouble adjusting, but all in all I'd say I'm fairly Americanized."

"Except for that accent."

He smiled. "Can't get rid of the accent now, can I? Then how would I ever attract the attention of pretty things like you?"

"By reading Shakespeare in a bar obviously."

He laughed, and the sound spread through my skin, loosening some of my nerves.

"You're cute," he said.

I rolled my eyes. "Yes . . . ridiculously so, as we established earlier."

"Would you feel better if I called you ridiculously sexy?"

Just like that, the ease I'd felt earlier disappeared, and my breaths came too shallow. I had no answer. What could I possibly say to that?

"What's that look for?" he asked.

I had no idea which of my multitude of emotions had shown on my face, so I shrugged.

"You act like no one's ever called you sexy before." That would be because they hadn't. "Which I know can't be true, not when you look the way you looked tonight. I could barely keep my hands off you, and we've only just met. I'd be embarrassed if I hadn't enjoyed it so much."

This was it. I may not have had sex, but I knew enough to know when a guy was putting the moves on me. And remarkably, I didn't even care. All I cared about was the fact that he was sitting so close to me and was driving me crazy. His hand was still leisurely stroking my ankle, and if he didn't kiss me again soon I was going to combust. "Look at me, I can't even keep my hands off you now."

I swallowed, but my mouth suddenly felt like I'd swallowed a sandbox.

He pulled himself up on his knees, and his hand trailed from my ankle up the outside of my uninjured calf. His hips were a few inches away from my knees as I sat there dumbfounded on the toilet.

"Tell me I'm not crazy," he said.

I couldn't do that. I was nowhere near sane enough at the moment to advise anyone else on rational behavior.

"Tell me I can kiss you."

That . . . *that* I could do.

"You can kiss—"

I didn't even finish the sentence before his lips were on mine and my burn was forgotten completely.

5

The kiss ended too soon.

An embarrassing groan of disappointment left my mouth, but it couldn't be helped. Luckily, Garrick wasn't done. He stood and pulled me up by my elbows. He drew me in until our bodies fit together in a way that hadn't been possible when I was seated.

"That's better," he said.

I didn't bother agreeing. I just lifted up on my tiptoes and kissed him.

Compared to our earlier kiss, this one was slow, exploratory, and like kindling on a fire. One of his hands curled around my neck, his thumb pressing gently into my collarbone. The other danced from my hair to my shoulder to my hip, and then back.

For once in my life, I concentrated simply on the feel of a guy against me, the brush of his tongue against mine, the pinpricks of heat where his fingers pressed into my skin. I didn't think about anything—not about my breath, or whether my hands were in the right place, or what he was expecting. I lost myself in him.

My hands rested at his hips, and I wanted to do some exploring of my own. I pulled my hands in until they rested on his stomach. At my movement, his lips pressed a little bit harder against mine. His tongue pushed a little bit deeper. I slid both hands up, feeling the hard curves of his body beneath the fabric of his shirt. When my exploration reached his chest, his hand tugged my hip forward, so that my stomach was pressed against him.

I could feel the way he wanted me, and a trickle of anxiety started at my spine. Then his kiss turned harder and faster, and I raced to follow his lead, ignoring my nerves.

I left one hand on his chest, wrapped the other around his neck, and pulled myself up farther on my tiptoes, so that my hips lined up with his.

Garrick broke the kiss and exhaled shakily against my lips. The brilliant blue I'd seen in his eyes earlier was overtaken almost completely by his black pupils. He placed a hand on my jaw; his thumb pulled at my bottom lip. For several long seconds, he just studied me.

"You *are* ridiculously sexy, you know."

I lowered my heels to the floor, my calves burning too much to stay on my tiptoes. And I couldn't look in his eyes anymore. Every time I'd almost completely turned off my brain, he said something to turn it back on. I said, "You know, you don't need that line. I was already kissing you."

"And what a good kiss it was." His thumb brushed against my lip again, and he tipped my face back up toward him. "I'd like to do it again somewhere that isn't your bathroom."

"Oh, right." Was he asking to go to my bedroom? I was pretty sure he was asking to go to my bedroom.

I fumbled with the doorknob for a few seconds before my clouded brain managed to swing the door open. We exited into the dark hallway again, and his hand found my back once more.

"Sorry, the hallway light is out, and I haven't had a chance to change it."

His lips were right by my ear when he answered, "I don't mind the dark."

All the tiny hairs along my skin stood on end.

We stepped into the living room, and I flipped on a light that actually worked. My apartment was a loft with an open floor plan. Two walls were brick, and the other was painted a pretty plum color. The ceiling was high, with exposed pipes crisscrossing above us. My bedroom was off to the right, separated from the living room by only a lavender curtain since I didn't actually have a door.

"Well, this is my living room." I gestured with one hand, unsure whether he expected a tour or if I should just skip straight to the bedroom. I'd never done this before, so I had no idea whether we were supposed to do the traditional niceties first. My heart raced wildly as he walked around the room, inspecting a painting here, a knickknack there.

"It's nice. Fits you, I think."

I beamed. I loved this apartment. It always made me feel like I was in an episode of *Friends*.

"I'm ashamed to say that my place is still covered in boxes. Wouldn't have made for a very interesting tour."

God, how I wished we were at his place. Then he would be in control. I hated not knowing what I was supposed to do next.

His eyes flicked to the curtain that led to my bedroom. It was quick. His eyes were almost immediately back on the lamp he was standing next to, but I saw it.

This was it. I was about to have sex.

Should I tell him I was a virgin? I should tell him.

Should I tell him now? Or right before?

I remembered Kelsey's advice and forced myself to dial back my fears. I turned the volume down so low that I could pretend I wasn't thinking at all.

Before I could chicken out, I walked forward and held out my hand. He took it immediately, and I led him through the curtain and into my bedroom. There was no overhead lighting in this area, so I flipped on a lamp to my right and then left him to turn on another beside my bed.

When I turned around, he was holding up the indecently short miniskirt that Kelsey had made me try on earlier.

His eyes met mine, and his grin made my lungs feel like they were on the verge of collapse. I snatched the skirt out of his hands, scooped up the few other articles of clothing still on my bed, and threw them into my closet.

"Sorry about that."

"You don't hear me complaining."

I raised an eyebrow and said, "Forget about it. You will never see me in that skirt."

"Never? Is that a challenge, love?"

"It's a promise."

He skirted the corner of my bed to join me in the space between my bed and the wall. "I'd feel very comfortable helping you break that promise."

He placed a hand on my shoulder, his index finger dipping beneath the strap of my tank top.

"I'm sure you'd be comfortable helping me do a lot of things."

His hand tightened on my shoulder, and his eyes dropped to my lips.

"That I would."

Then he kissed me.

He didn't bother with soft and sweet this time. There was a hungry desperation in his kiss that had me gasping into his mouth. His teeth pulled on my bottom lip in the same way his thumb had earlier, and my whole body trembled in response. He bent slightly and swept an arm around my waist, pulling me up and against him so that our bodies were lined up perfectly.

My toes barely brushed the floor, but it didn't matter. He was holding me up. I buried my hands in his messy locks and threw myself into the kiss. He took a few steps backward and sat on the edge of my bed. On instinct, my legs went on either side of his lap, straddling him. The hand that had been around my waist curved around my butt and pulled me against him.

If I'd had any doubt about where this was heading,

it disappeared then. He pulled me in again, his own hips tilting up at the same time, and I broke the kiss, gasping. His mouth skimmed across my jaw and down my neck. His lips lingered over my pulse point, his tongue brushing across the sensitive skin. He continued down over my collarbone until my tank top blocked any further progress. I thought he would stop, but he slipped the tank top strap off my shoulder, and his lips never left my skin. His other hand snuck beneath the bottom of my shirt, teasing the skin around the waistband of my skirt.

My hands were still tangled in his hair, and I tightened my grip and pulled his face back to mine. His hand brushed higher as we kissed, smoothing over my rib cage, my skin burning in his wake. When his hand cupped my breast, I rocked against him, and he groaned. The skirt I'd thrown on earlier was up around my thighs, and there was so little between us. I tilted my hips forward again, and this time it was me who moaned. When his other hand found the edge of my shirt, it was to pull it up and over my head.

We broke our kiss to let the fabric pass between us. I resisted the urge to cover myself as his gaze raked over me. And God was I thankful that Kelsey had insisted I wear some cute lingerie. This particular set was black and white lace.

When he looked at me, it was with such obvious desire that I knew he didn't care about that little pudge that had stressed me out earlier. His right hand kneaded my breast gently, while his left found my neck. He pulled my face close to his. I thought he was going to kiss me again, but at the last second he swerved, and he pressed his cheek against mine. He dropped a kiss on the edge of my jaw, just below my ear.

And God did that feel amazing. It was just a small innocent kiss, but it had me gripping his hair and pushing my hips down against his. His lips brushed against the shell of my ear as he whispered, "Did I say ridiculously sexy? I meant *unbelievably* sexy."

I was unbelievably turned on.

He kissed me again and then turned and laid me back against the bed. He paused to pull his shirt over his head, and for the first time I got to see the hard planes of his body that had fascinated me earlier. He rose up on his knees, my legs still splayed on either side of him. He stopped to study me again.

This was the part where I should tell him. I should just say it. Just spit it out.

I'm a virgin.

Just three words.

Not that hard, right?

I swallowed and cleared my throat.

Then he ducked his head and pressed his lips against the skin of my stomach, and all my thoughts disappeared.

6

It was possible that I might not make it to the sex. With the
way he was mapping out my body with his lips—I was going
to spontaneously combust before we ever got that far.

His fingers trailed up my thighs and stroked the skin of
my hip just below the waistband of my panties. Something in
my brain detonated, and panic filled me.

I was going to be so terrible at this . . . the worst he'd ever
had probably. And then he'd never want to see me again (and
I *really* wanted to see him again). I'd probably be traumatized
and never want to have sex again, which meant every relationship for the rest of my life would fail, and I would end up
alone and miserable with nine cats and a ferret.

I didn't want to end up alone and miserable with nine cats and a ferret.

Then one of his hands pushed my panties to the side, and I was anything but miserable.

Black danced around the edges of my vision, and all the feeling in my body seemed to narrow to that one spot where he was touching me, and holy heart failure, it felt amazing. His fingers hit a spot inside me that had me arching up and toward him. His head dipped, and he started dropping kisses across my chest.

My hands had a mind of their own as they kneaded at his back and then slipped around to his stomach, where I flicked open the button on his jeans. He made a sound in the back of his throat, and his lips crashed against mine. He kissed me fiercely, pressing me down into the mattress. The kisses kept building—harder and faster—and I needed something more. I slid my hand along the taut skin of his stomach to the front of his jeans. Then his lips broke from mine with a groan. He didn't pull back, but kept his lips millimeters from mine. His breath came out in a rush.

"Oh God, Bliss . . ."

He placed a final lingering kiss on my lips and then pulled back until he was kneeling above me. I heard the metal clink of his zipper and kept my eyes focused on the frame of his shoulders as he fiddled with his clothes. He stood for a few seconds, and I fixed my eyes on the ceiling. I wanted this. Badly.

I was about to repeat my mantra again when his lips and hands came back to me—frenzied, almost desperate.

I could feel the pressure building low in my core, and

every muscle in my legs was pulled tight as I waited for what I knew was coming.

Then he dragged my panties down my legs, and his body settled into the crook of my thighs, and it was like I'd just been submerged in ice.

I was about to have sex.

With a guy I'd just met, who I knew absolutely nothing about.

And *he* knew nothing about *me* . . . including the fact that I was a virgin.

And God, I wanted to go through with it. I was sick of being a virgin, and he was unbelievably sexy, but this wasn't me.

I couldn't do this. Not with him.

I just . . . couldn't.

I froze up beneath him, but his mouth continued worshiping at the juncture between my neck and shoulder.

I should have told him I was a virgin or that I wasn't ready. It wouldn't have been pretty or easy, but at least he would have understood . . . probably.

Instead, my eyes locked on the porcelain cat cookie jar I'd inherited from my great grandmother, and my brain created a ridiculous excuse out of the first thing that came to my mind.

"Stop! Cats! Stop . . ."

What the hell was I saying?

I put the heels of my palms against his shoulders and pushed up slightly.

He pulled back, his eyes dark, his hair mussed, and his lips swollen from our kisses. I almost changed my mind then. He looked almost irresistible. Almost.

"Sorry, did you say cats?"

"Yes, I can't do this . . . right now. Because . . . I have a cat. Yes, I have a cat that I need to, um, get? Take care of! I have to take care of my cat! So . . . I can't do *this*." I gestured between us, hoping to God that I didn't sound as crazy to him as I sounded to myself. Improbable.

I don't even have a cat!

I don't know what synapses misfired in my brain, but I wanted to kick myself. I wanted to punch myself in the face until I lost consciousness. Right about then I probably could have dived into a pool of hydrochloric acid without even a pep talk.

His brain must have been as clouded as mine, because he paused for a few moments, processing, then looked around.

"I don't see a cat."

My throat was getting dry, the way it always does when I lie. I am a terrible liar (as evidenced by, well, me).

"That's because . . . it's not here. Yes. The cat that I own is not here because . . . I have to go get her. I forgot, I was supposed to go pick her up."

He glanced at the clock, which now read 12:20 A.M.

"You're supposed to pick her up now?"

I pushed at him again, and this time he rolled off of me and to the side easily. He was completely naked, and I was in my bra and skirt with my panties still hooked around one ankle.

"Yes . . . she's at the vet! It's a, um, twenty-four-hour veterinarian. . . ."

"A twenty-four-hour veterinarian?"

"Uh, yeah. We have those here . . . in America. Totally."

That hydrochloric acid was sounding incredibly appealing right now. "And I was supposed to pick her up hours ago."

"You can't go by in the morning?"

I tried to slip my panties back on my other foot, and I toppled backward, ass-planting on my hardwood floor.

"Jesus, Bliss!"

He hopped off the bed and knelt beside me, which only made me more flustered considering he was *still* naked and *still,* um, ready.

"I'm fine, promise. I'm fine. I just . . . if I don't pick her up tonight, there will be a fee, and I can't afford it."

"Well, let me get dressed and I'll go with you."

"*No!* Um, no, that's okay. Shouldn't your locksmith be coming soon?" I finished with a smile that I hoped said, *This is no big deal.* I'm sure it actually looked like *I'm a crazy person, run now while you can!*

He glanced at the clock, his gorgeous face marred by a frown.

"I guess, yeah."

"Great. I'm just—I'm just going to run. You can, um, let yourself out whenever you're. . . ."

My eyes wandered over his body again, and I felt like melting into a puddle of idiocy and mortification and arousal.

". . . whenever you're, um, ready. Um, done. Um, just whenever you like."

Then I flew through the curtain that shielded my bedroom from the rest of the apartment and bolted out the door, ignoring him as he called out my name.

It wasn't until I'd walked halfway across the parking lot that I realized:

1. I wasn't wearing shoes.
    A. Or a shirt.
2. I didn't bring my keys.
    A. Or anything really.
3. I'd just left a complete stranger in my apartment.
    A. Naked.

Whoever said one-night stands were supposed to be simple with no strings attached had clearly never met the disaster that was me.

F our.

That's the number of people who saw me hiding around the corner from my own apartment in just a skirt and a bra.

Eleven.

That's the number of ant bites I got on my shoeless feet.

Twenty-seven.

That's the number of times I was tempted to do myself physical harm because I am an *idiot*.

One.

That's the number of times I tried not to cry, but failed.

Garrick stayed in my apartment for a good ten minutes

after I left. The entire time my mind was like a five-year-old who just drank a bathtub full of energy drinks. What was he doing in there? Was he just getting dressed *reeeaaally* slowly? Was he looking through my things? Was he trashing my place because I'd run out and left him there like the biggest jerk this side of Kanye West at the 2009 VMAs?

When he finally exited, I watched him close my door, and then pause. He looked at the metal apartment number nailed into the siding and just stared at it for a while. Then he shook his head and started toward his own apartment.

I waited until I couldn't see him anymore, and then I waited for another five minutes just to be safe (six more ant bites, one more passerby, and four visions of self-harm later).

As soon as I got inside I curled up on my bed. The same bed where I'd almost had sex. The same bed where I had *wanted* to have sex . . . sort of. The same bed that had held an incredibly sexy, incredibly naked British boy. Perhaps I had just jumped off the cliff into crazy town, but I could swear that the comforter was still warm where his body had been. Like a complete psycho, I leaned my face into the pillow and sniffed like girls in books and movies always do to see if I could still catch his scent.

I couldn't. And I felt super-creepy.

I also couldn't sleep in this bed without going crazy.

I moved my pillow to the couch, where I sat numbly, probably in shock. At the very least, I could reassure myself that this was only a private humiliation. No one else had to know how pathetic I was. And after my borderline schizophrenic display earlier, I was pretty sure he was going to avoid me as avidly as I planned on avoiding him. We might live in the same apartment complex, but if I had my way we'd never have to see each other again.

Morning came too early, and I was stiff from sleeping on my crappy couch for the entire night. Plus, my head was pounding like I actually had punched myself in the face like I'd been tempted to do the night before.

Stupid tequila.

I moved sluggishly, dragging myself into and out of the shower at a much slower pace than normal. My hair was still wet when there came a knock on my door. Kelsey practically fell on top of me when I opened the door because she'd been trying to peek through the peephole.

Silently, she smiled and mouthed, "Is he still here?"

I sighed and said, "No, Kels, he's gone." I turned away from her, grabbing my head to try to stop the turning that was happening in there too. I left the door open and walked away, knowing she'd come in whether or not I issued an invitation.

"Someone's a crabby camper this morning. What is it? Was it awful? Was he like . . . minuscule?"

"He was not minuscule!" Not that I had a great deal to compare it to, but I was pretty positive that wasn't the case.

"Oh, so it was just bad?"

I should have just told her that I hadn't gone through with it, but my head was pounding, my stomach was churning, and I did *not* want to be forced into going out again tonight for try number two.

So I lied.

"He was fine. I'm just hungover."

"Fine? *Fine?* Come on, that boy was gorgeous! Please at least pretend that you liked it!"

"I did like it!" If by "it" we were talking about the single greatest make-out session of my life. "I liked him."

Those words were out of my mouth before I really thought of the consequences.

"Oh no!" Kelsey cried. "No, you don't! I know he was your first and all, but that does not mean you have to jump into insta-love. This was purely physical. That's it. If you try to do something stupid like marry this boy, I will personally drag you kicking and screaming away from the altar."

"No! You're right of course." I shrugged like it was no big deal, but my throat was getting dry, and I could feel the skin of my neck and cheeks getting red. I hoped she would just assume I was embarrassed, because normally she could pick out my lies like nobody's business. "I swear it's not a big deal. I'm not in love with him. I'm not going to *marry* him. In fact, I barely remember most of it." And by "barely remember" I mean most of it didn't actually happen. The rest, though . . . that was imprinted on my brain. Not even the almighty tequila could take those memories away from me. I just wish it had taken the memories of how it ended.

"Well, that sucks. But everything was okay, right?"

"Yeah." I forced a smile. "Everything is okay."

Kelsey hugged me, and it felt like one of those moments when we were supposed to be bonding or connecting or thinking about the same thing, but since everything on my side was a lie, I just hugged her back and tried to pretend she was comforting me about my awkwardness.

"All right, now get your ass in gear. If I don't get coffee

before class, I'm going to die. My sleep schedule is still off from Christmas break, and I feel like a freaking zombie."

"Zombie" for Kelsey meant she was at a 6 on the perky scale instead of a 10.

I always thought I was an extrovert until I became a theatre major. Then I realized I just didn't like silence. When there were plenty of other people around willing to be the entertaining one, I found I much preferred just observing.

The Starbucks on campus was overrun with a zombie horde of other sleep-deprived students. By the time I got my caramel macchiato, I was pretty much already awake, and we were definitely going to be late for the first class of the last semester of our last year of college.

We raced to the fine arts building, breezing past the hipster art majors smoking outside the doors. We jogged down the hallway to find that, sure enough, the doors to the small black box theatre where we had acting class were already closed.

"Shipoopi," Kelsey said.

Then, because we're theatre majors, we broke into the song from *The Music Man*. Because sometimes life just needs a little music. (But we did it quietly and on fast-forward because we *were* still late for class.)

There was no way to enter this theatre without making a ridiculous amount of noise. The doors creaked and slammed no matter what you did. We pushed open one of the doors and immediately heard Eric Barnes, the head of the department, say, "Late!"

We called out an automatic "Sorry, Eric!"

Careful not to spill our coffees, we pushed through the

curtains that surrounded the edge of the room and grabbed the nearest empty seats on the risers.

I set my coffee down and went about organizing my stuff, digging through my bag for a pen and my folder.

"As I was saying," Eric continued, "Ben Jackson was supposed to be teaching this course." Ben was pretty much our favorite teacher, but he'd been offered a role in this killer new show off Broadway and would be taking the semester off. "But as you all know, he's in New York for a few months. To replace him for the time being, we have one of our most talented former students—Mr. Taylor."

I finally found a dull pencil in the bottom of my purse. It would have to do. Kelsey chose that minute to grab my elbow and jerk me toward her. I glanced up at her and then at the front of the class where she was looking. Then the pencil I'd worked so hard to find fell from my hand and rolled away, lost to the abyss under the risers.

The new professor was staring at me, even though everyone was clapping and he probably should have been waving or at the very least smiling. Our eyes met, and suddenly I was very glad I'd already set down my coffee.

Because the new professor had been naked in my bed a mere eight hours before.

Garrick was my teacher.

8

It felt like hours passed before he looked away from me. When he did, the smile he gave the class was uneasy, and he tugged absentmindedly at the tie around his neck.

"Thank you, Eric. But please, everyone, call me Garrick."

I thought I could actually feel the hormones released into the atmosphere when the girls in the room heard his accent. I felt Kelsey staring at me, but I fixed my eyes on one of the stage lights hanging overhead and tried to think my rapidly beating heart into submission. This was bad. This was *so bad.*

"Like Eric said, I did my undergrad here, and then graduated this past May with an MFA in acting from Temple University in Philadelphia. I'd been working in the theatre scene there for about six months when Eric called and asked if I'd be interested in the temporary position here."

I glanced at him out of the corner of my eye, simultaneously anticipating and dreading the thought of making eye contact with him. He was not looking at me. In fact, his whole body was angled toward the students on the other side of the room, pretty much ignoring the entire section where I was seated. Other than the fact that he was pointedly not looking at one side of the room, there was no sign that he was worried or frazzled in any way, whereas I could feel the heat in my cheeks, and my hands were shaking as I pressed them into my knees.

"I loved my four years here, and I'm, uh . . ."

He glanced at me, and I could do nothing but look back—wide-eyed and petrified. He cleared his throat and returned his gaze to the other side of the room.

"I'm really excited to be back."

I wanted to crawl into a hole and die.

I wanted to crawl into a hole at the bottom of a ravine, be buried under an avalanche, and then die.

I wanted . . . to cry.

Eric excused himself then to let us get to know our new teacher. I wished I could excuse myself too because I happened to already know him plenty well.

"Well, then," Garrick started. "I realize that I'm not that much older than you lot." Another flick of his eyes to mine. It was becoming nearly impossible to swallow.

"But my goal here is to provide you with some insight into the next step in your journey from someone who isn't so far removed. We all love Eric, Ben, Kate, and the rest of the faculty, but let's face it, they're not exactly the youngest kids on the block." The whole class laughed. I was too busy concentrating on not throwing up. "It was a different world when they started their careers. When I was sitting where you are, we called this class Senior Prep; I think now it's called the Business of Theatre. In it, we'll be covering everything from auditions to career options to Actors' Equity. We'll also spend some time talking about the more abstract side of things. Because I hate to break it to you guys, but the hardest part about this business isn't landing roles or making ends meet, though that is difficult. The hardest thing is keeping up your spirits and remembering why you chose this in the first place."

He didn't have to try too hard to scare us about our futures. We were all already operating on threat level orange. We'd been having middle-of-the-night, soul-searching conversations (while drunk, of course) since the year started.

"Now, if you don't mind, I'd like to hear a bit about you all. Why don't you tell me your names and what you're interested in doing after you graduate."

There were about twenty in the class. The first eight or so all recited their names followed by the obligatory "I'm moving to New York."

When you're an actor, moving to New York is pretty much the dream. Those who are lucky can actually make it the plan. Some of us have to think a little more realistically.

Cade, my best friend besides Kelsey, said, "Cade Winston. At the moment I'm a little torn between grad school and just going straight into auditioning. I can't really tell if I actually *want* to go to grad school or if I'm just scared."

Garrick smiled, and even though I was freaking out, I smiled too. I felt like that about a lot of things in my life . . . not just acting.

He said, "Good. That's honest, Cade. And the more honest you can be with yourself the better. Hopes and dreams are great, but they are a lot easier to break than a solid plan. We'll see if we can't figure out exactly what you want while you're in this class."

After that, it was like everyone felt okay to say what we were actually thinking instead of what we felt was expected of us.

We had spent so much time defending our choice to do theatre that it had become hard to show any vulnerability at all. There's only so many times you can handle someone asking about your fallback for when things don't work out before you start thinking that maybe the fallback should just be your plan.

Sometimes I wished I were a bit more like Kelsey. She was practically fearless. Though I guess it's easy to be a little fearless when your family is loaded.

"Kelsey Summers. I'm taking a year off to travel and just explore before I decide on what I'm doing. People always say that the most interesting actors are interesting people, so I figure it's a good investment to spend some time becoming more fascinating than I already am."

"Diva," I muttered under my breath.

She narrowed her eyes and delivered a quick pinch to the back of my arm in response. I yelped and nearly toppled out of my seat just as Garrick turned his eyes on me and said, "And you?"

Rubbing at my arm, I had to look away from his eyes before I could answer.

"Bliss Edwards. I'm a little torn between acting and stage management. And since they don't really offer master's programs where you can do both, I think I'll just go ahead and enter the, um, job market or whatever."

I looked back at him, but his eyes had already moved on to Dom, who was sitting one row above me.

I closed my eyes and took a deep breath. Kelsey's hand found mine, and she squeezed.

It took another twenty minutes to finish up introductions because, well, we're theatre people. We love to hear ourselves talk.

With only five minutes left in class, Garrick said, "Great. It sounds like you've all at least given a thought to the next step. Wednesday I want you all to come to class with your résumé and headshots and be ready to audition."

"For what?" Dom asked. "It's the first week of class. There aren't any auditions for a few weeks." Dom loved to hear himself speak more than most.

"It doesn't matter," Garrick answered. "In the real world, you might go to ten auditions in a day. You might have weeks to prepare or you might have an hour. Your job is acting only if you land the part. Until then, your job is auditioning, so you better be good at it. Dismissed. See you all on Wednesday."

His grin as he said this wasn't quite as awe-inspiring as the grins he'd worn last night, but it was still enough to make my steps stutter on my way down the risers.

I was at the curtains, a mere ten feet away from the door,

when I heard "Miss Edwards, can I speak to you for a moment?"

Kelsey's face was caught somewhere between pity and glee. For the first time in twelve hours, I wanted to punch someone besides myself.

"Lunch at noon?" she asked. I nodded, even though I wasn't sure I would survive until noon. Hell, I wasn't even sure I could stomach going to my next class.

I took my time walking toward him, waiting for the rest of the class to clear. Dom was currently bombarding Garrick with questions, so I took a second to distract myself with Cade. Where Kelsey was the friend who dragged me out to bars and encouraged stupid behavior, Cade was the friend who always knew the right thing to say.

Cade's first words: "On a scale of one to bitchy, how hungover are you?"

I raised the corner of my mouth in a smile. That was all I could manage in my vortex of emotions, but it was a smile all the same. "Depends . . . right now? A solid seven. If Dom tries to talk to me . . . we're going to need a bigger scale."

He laughed, and something made me wonder how last night would have gone if I'd told Cade my secret instead of Kelsey. Somehow I doubt things would have turned out the same.

"I gotta run. Poli-sci." He made a face, and I concurred, glad I'd gotten that out of the way last year. "Let's do something tonight, okay?"

"Sure." This time I did smile, because Cade was great for distractions, and that was most definitely what I needed right then.

He pecked me on the cheek and then went on his way.

I turned toward Garrick to find him watching me, his eyes dark and narrowed. Dom was long gone. He must have gone out the doors on the other side. We stood there awkwardly for several seconds. His hands were shoved in his pockets, and mine were fidgeting with the bag slung across my shoulders.

Finally, he cleared his throat.

"How's your leg?"

I swallowed and looked down at my legs. I'd worn a skirt today to keep it uncovered. I tilted my leg so he could see the bandage. "Good. I rebandaged it this morning. It's blistered, but as far as I can tell, or, well, according to the Internet, that's normal."

I looked back, but his eyes were still on my legs.

I stiffened. God, this was so awkward.

He cleared his throat again.

"So . . . you're in college."

"So . . . you're not."

He stayed still for another second, then turned to the side abruptly, pacing several feet away from me, and then back. His fingers pushed through his hair in frustration, and all I could think about was my own fingers in his hair and how incredibly soft it had been.

"I thought—" he started. "Well, I wasn't doing much thinking at all. But you don't look like you're in college. I said I went to school here, and that I'd just moved back, and you said, 'Me too,' so I just assumed you had done the same."

I kept having this irrational need to blink. I wasn't crying or anything, but I just couldn't stop. I said, "I lived in Texas when I was really young. I meant that I moved back here for school."

He nodded once, and then kept nodding. So he was nodding, and I was blinking, and neither of us was saying what really needed to be said.

And since I couldn't stand silence, I was the first to break.

"I won't tell anyone." His eyebrows raised, but I couldn't tell if it was surprise or judgment or just a facial tic. "I mean, not that there's anything . . . not that we . . . I mean, we didn't actually . . . um, make the beast with two backs and all that."

Oh. My. God.

Killmenowkillmenowkillmenowkillmenooooooow.

The beast with two backs? Seriously?

I'm twenty-two years old, and rather than just spitting out the word "sex," I used a Shakespeare reference! A really *embarrassing* Shakespeare reference.

And he was smiling! And his smile did funny things to my insides that had me thinking about last night, which was totally not something I needed to be thinking about right now. No beasts. No backs. No last night.

I looked away, trying to keep it together. I took a deep breath and said, as calmly as I could, "This doesn't have to be a big deal."

He took a moment to answer, and I wondered if he was waiting for me to look at him. If he was, he'd be waiting for a while.

"You're right. We're both adults. We can just forget it happened."

There was no way I could forget it happened. But I could pretend.

I could act.

"Right," I nodded.

I turned to leave, but his voice stopped me.

"How's your cat?"

"What cat? Oh! *My cat.* The cat . . . that is mine. Oh, she's . . ." I had said it was a she, right? ". . . She's fine. All meowing and purring and other cat things."

God, why did the door have to be so far away?

I kept walking away, calling back my last few words over my shoulder.

"I've got to get to class. I'll see you Wednesday I guess. Okay, bye!"

I speed-walked out the door, down the hallway into the art wing, past the ceramics classroom, and into the handicapped-accessible bathroom that no one ever used. Then I sank down to my knees. (On a *bathroom floor.* Clearly I was distraught because . . . *gross.*)

I focused on not hyperventilating. Only I could have an affair with a teacher by accident. I knew one thing for sure. There was no way in hell I was going to my next class.

9

I swear there was so much awkward in the air, it felt practically solid."

My face was pressed against the table in the student lounge while Kelsey tried to ply me with French fries and other wonderful carbohydrates.

She patted my back halfheartedly. There was nothing even remotely mothering about Kelsey, but at least she was trying. "You're exaggerating, Bliss. The only thing I felt in the air was sexual tension. I mean, he didn't look at you often, but when he did. . . . Hello! Swoon!"

"There is no way I can survive a semester in that class."

"That's ridiculous. You're an actor. Actors sleep with

each other all the time, and then move on. Hell, don't you remember freshman year when you didn't want to make out with Dom in that scene, and Eric sent you in the other room and told you to kiss until you guys were comfortable with each other?"

"Why would you bring up what is, as of today, the second most mortifying moment of my life?"

She rolled her eyes. "Because you got over it."

"I will never get over having Dom's tongue down my throat. I can still taste the douchiness."

"You will be fine, Bliss. It's five months. And you only have to see him for three hours a week. It will be over before you know it. Then you can jump his bones one more time before you travel the world with me."

"There are so many crazy things in that statement that I don't even know where to begin."

"You will begin by eating, or we'll be late for Directing."

Grumbling, I shoved a few fries in my mouth to appease her.

She rummaged around in her purse for her phone, but her hands closed around something else. "Oh, I forgot. I have Advil . . . you want some?"

I swallowed and said, "Why would I want that?"

She quirked her head to the side. "Aren't you sore after . . . you know . . . getting your freak on?"

Stupid Bliss. So freaking stupid.

"Oh! Oh, right. No, no, I'm fine. I took a bunch this morning. I'm good, thanks."

"Thatta girl."

I moved through the rest of the day on autopilot, ready

to get home and crawl into the cocoon of forgetting that is sleep. I didn't even bother taking off my clothes before I fell into bed.

My phone woke me a few hours later. It was Cade.

"Hey, babe—you ready to hang out?"

I peered blearily at the clock PM. It was only seven o' clock.

I yawned. "Yeah . . . sure. What did you have in mind?"

"Well, I was thinking—"

"No drinking," I cut him off. "I cannot handle any drinking."

He laughed. "No hair of the dog for you? Fine . . . Lindsay's playing tonight at Grind. How does coffee sound?"

I yawned again. Lindsay was a fellow theatre major. A night listening to her music would be simple and mellow. Exactly what I needed. "Coffee sounds perfect."

When I walked outside twenty minutes later, I swung my head from side to side, paranoid that I'd run into Garrick. When I was certain no one was around, I jogged into the parking lot and climbed into Cade's beat-up old Honda.

He greeted me with a smile. I resisted the urge to glance back in the direction of Garrick's apartment.

"I forgot to mention earlier that you looked great today. I mean, minus that lovely hungover quality. You never wear skirts to class."

I wanted to say, "Just drive already!" But that would have sounded crazy even for me. So I answered, "Oh, I burned my leg, and I'm not supposed to wear tight clothing over it."

"Seriously?" he asked. "What happened?"

I couldn't exactly tell him the real reason. Because then

he'd want to know whose motorcycle it had been and why I had been with that person and yadda-yadda.

"Oh, I burned it with my straightener."

"You burned your leg with your straightener? How long is your leg hair?"

You'd think after all the lying I'd done in the past twenty-four hours that I would have been getting slightly better at it. You would be wrong.

"Ha-ha. So funny!" I grimaced. "I knocked it off the counter, you punk, and it hit my leg."

I fiddled with the air-conditioning vent even though it barely worked in his piece-of-junk car.

"Just don't drop your coffee on yourself. Or better yet . . . get iced coffee."

I said, "Aye, aye, captain."

Grind was a cute little house on the edge of campus that had been turned into a coffeehouse a few years before. Inside you ordered coffee, and outside there was a veranda where they hosted live music on most nights. The inside was packed. I sent Cade outside to find seats and told him I'd get the drinks. I got an iced café mocha for me and a smoothie for Cade. He didn't even like coffee, but he came there for me.

I stood in line for ten or fifteen minutes, so by the time I headed outside I had no idea where Cade was. I strolled past the tables, nodding at people I knew, avoiding eye contact with those I didn't. I caught Lindsay's eye up onstage as she was setting up, and she grinned.

Finally I spotted Cade standing by a table up near the front. It was an awesome spot considering how packed this place was.

I came up behind him and nudged my elbow into his back.

"Jesus, Cade, I thought I'd never find you out here. Couldn't you have at least texted?"

Cade glanced over his shoulder at me, then wrapped his arm around my shoulder and took the smoothie from my left hand.

"Sorry, babe, I was talking and got distracted. Look who it is!"

He pulled me forward, and there was Garrick.

This time I wasn't lucky enough to have already put down my coffee. So when I saw Garrick, it slipped out of my hand and splashed all over my feet.

Cade, with his super-fast reflexes, narrowly dodged getting it all over his Toms.

"Holy crap, Bliss. I was joking about the iced coffee, but I'm glad you listened. I swear you didn't used to be this clumsy."

I still couldn't speak. My feet were cold and sticky. And my face felt way too hot.

"Here," Cade said. "Sit down. Mr. Taylor said we could share his table."

"It's Garrick, Cade." I'm sure he'd told Cade that half a dozen times already.

Cade ignored him and turned to me. "I'll run inside and get you some napkins. You want another drink?"

"No, no. I'm good, Cade. You stay. I'll go clean up."

"Forget it. You like Lindsay's music much more than I do. All 'be the change' and 'girl power' stuff. I don't want you to miss it. Sit." This time his hands pushed down on my shoulders until my butt hit the seat. Then he was off, and I was left alone with Garrick again.

"What are you doing here?" My question came out angry.

By comparison, he was sweet and calm, and possibly a little sad. "My Internet still isn't hooked up at the apartment, and I needed to check my email. I can go, if you'd like."

Yes.

"No," I sighed. "I'm not going to run you off. I just wish you hadn't invited us to sit with you."

"Well, Cade didn't say he was here with you. I was just trying to be nice."

"I'm sorry . . . I just . . . this is awkward. Cade doesn't know—"

"—I'm not going to tell him, if that's what you're worried about. I'd like to keep this job, and besides, your personal life is none of my business. What happened between us is over."

His voice turned hard as he spoke. Over? Why did that feel like a punch to the stomach? His teeth were clenched, drawing my eyes to the strong, smooth line of his jaw.

"You shaved," I said. Clearly, no filter.

His jaw unclenched, and he looked at me in confusion. "Uh, yes, I did."

We sat in silence, and I just couldn't get myself to stop looking at him. His eyes were ocean water blue, and without the scruff he looked younger, less rugged sexy and more boy-next-door hotness.

His eyes dropped to my lips, and I realized I was biting down on the bottom one. God, I wanted to kiss him again.

I sprang up from my seat. "This was a bad idea. I'm going to go. Tell Cade I got sick or something."

He stood too. "No, Bliss, wait. I'm sorry. Don't leave. I'll . . . shit, I don't know what I'll do. I'll just sit here quietly, and you two can ignore me completely. I promise."

At that moment, Lindsay stepped back up onto the small makeshift stage, and the lights came on, and people clapped.

If I was going to leave, I needed to do it now. If I got up in the middle of the set, Lindsay would see and she'd be pissed.

So, against my better judgment, I sat back down.

Garrick kept his promise and kept his eyes glued to his screen. I sat quietly as Lindsay did her sound check, my neck strained tightly to resist looking at him.

Cade arrived back right as Lindsay was introducing herself.

"Hey," he whispered. "Randy was busing, and he let me borrow a towel. I figured this would be better than a bunch of napkins."

Then he lifted one of my sticky feet into his lap, removed my shoe, and started wiping down my leg with the damp towel. I giggled when he passed a particularly ticklish section.

I heard Garrick stop typing.

On instinct alone, I looked at him, but he was looking at Cade . . . and at my legs. I cleared my throat and pulled my foot back. I took the towel from Cade and said, "Thanks, but I think I can get this. I don't trust you not to tickle me."

Garrick went back to his computer, Cade focused on Lindsay, and I ducked my head down to get a closer look at my feet. When I was sure they weren't looking, I clenched my eyes shut and let out a silent scream. A real scream would have felt better, but I would take what I could get.

I recognized Lindsay's first few songs, having heard her play several times before, both on the stage and just in the greenroom during rehearsals and between classes. She had this great, raw, acoustic sound, and her lyrics were always some kind of social commentary, calling people on their bullshit. Which was why, when she leaned in to the mike and introduced her next song, I was so incredibly surprised.

"This next one is a little bit different for me. The lovely owner of this establishment . . ." (she pointed off to the side) ". . . wave Kenny . . ." (he looked under duress, but he waved) ". . . anyway, Kenny made a request that I play at least one song that wasn't . . . how did you put it, Kenny? 'Bitter or political' I believe is what he said. And since I'm incapable of writing anything like that, I'm singing a song written by a friend of mine who wishes to remain anonymous. It's called 'Resist.'"

The song opened gently, with a simple progression of chords, similar to Lindsay's normal sound. Then it turned, became mournful, passionate, almost desperate. She sang . . . and I wished I had left when I had the chance.

> *No matter how close, you are always too far*
> *My eyes are drawn everywhere you are*

The quiet conversations that had been happening stopped. It was such a dramatic change that all eyes fixed on her. But I could *swear* that I felt one pair of eyes on me.

> *I'm tired of the way we both pretend,*
> *Tired of always wanting and never giving in.*

I can feel it in my skin, see it in your grin.
We're more. We always have been.

Think of everything we've missed.
Every touch and every kiss.
Because we both insist.
Resist.

His gaze was a physical weight pressing against my skin. My heart thudded quickly in my chest, and my breaths came shorter. I didn't want to resist. I couldn't help it. I looked.

Hold your breath and close your eyes.
Distract yourself with other guys.
It's no surprise, your defeated sighs,
Aren't you tired of the lies?

But he wasn't looking at me. He wasn't typing, but his eyes were fixed on his computer, and he seemed . . . unaware. Was it just me? Was I imagining it all?

Think of everything we've missed.
Every touch and every kiss.
Because we both insist.
Resist.

No matter how close, you are always too far.
My eyes are drawn everywhere you are.

Suddenly I didn't want to be there anymore. I couldn't be this close to him. I was going to go crazy. It was stupid . . . even more stupid than having a one-night stand would have been, but I *liked* him. He didn't like Shakespeare, and he rode a motorcycle, and he was my teacher . . . but I *liked* him.

> *I'm done. I won't ignore.*
> *I won't pretend or resist.*
> *I want more.*

10

Lindsay finished out the last few chords, then stuck her tongue out and said, "Blech. Happy, Kenny?"

Cade laughed and gave a loud whoop. The crowd started clapping and whistling. I tried to raise my hands to join, but they were like lead in my lap.

I looked at Garrick, and this time he was looking at me. His eyes were dark, and when we connected, he made no effort to look away. Maybe I hadn't been imagining his stare earlier. We watched each other as the clapping died down, and for the first time in my entire life I really *understood* that "heart beating out of your chest" thing because it felt like there was something inside of me desperate to get out.

Before I went crazy, I ripped my eyes away, stood, and pulled Cade up by his elbow.

"Hey, what's up?" He was so good at reading me, and I watched as his eyes went from amused to concerned. "Everything okay?"

"Yeah, of course. I'm just tired. Can you take me home?"

"Sure, of course." He pressed a hand to my cheek like he was my mother checking my temperature. He barely took his eyes off me as he said, "Thanks for letting us share your table, Mr. Taylor. See you Wednesday."

"It's Garrick, Cade, please. You two have a good night."

Garrick looked only at Cade as he spoke, which was probably for the best. With an arm wrapped around my shoulder, I let my friend lead me out an archway on the side of the property that led to the parking lot.

I'd never been so glad to climb into a rusty car that smelled faintly of oil and cheese. Cade climbed in beside me. "You sure you're okay?"

"Yeah, I promise, I'm just tired."

"Okay." He didn't look convinced. "Let's get you home then."

He turned the key, and nothing happened. No engine, no lights, nothing.

"Aww . . . shit."

"What?" I asked. "What does that mean?"

"It means my car is a piece of crap."

He turned the key again, and when nothing happened, he slammed a palm into the steering wheel. I pulled my legs up into the seat and laid my head against my knees.

"Hold on a sec." Cade climbed out of the car and popped

the hood. I stayed curled up in my seat trying to mentally erase the last twenty-four hours from my brain. Somewhere between analyzing every look Garrick had given me tonight and planning out what I would say and how I would act in our next class, I must have fallen asleep.

The next thing I knew Cade was shaking me awake, and the car was definitely still not on.

I rubbed at my eyes and climbed from the car.

"Sorry, I guess I was even more tired than I thought."

"Listen, we can't get the car started, and we've tried everything we can think of."

My brain didn't register the "we" until the hood started lowering, and Cade was still standing beside me.

And of course, there was Garrick *again*. Because the world just couldn't make anything easier on me.

"We even tried jump-starting it using Mr. Taylor's bike."

"I told you, it's Garrick, Cade."

"Yeah, yeah, I know. So anyway, since I don't live far away. . . ."

Oh Lord. No. Please no. Cade was an RA in one of the dorms, which meant he could walk home. I, on the other hand, lived a few miles from campus.

"I asked Mr. Taylor, and he said he could give you a ride home. Turns out you guys even live in the same apartment complex."

"You don't say." I tried to turn my gritted teeth into a smile. "That's nice of him, but I can just call Kelsey to come get me. It's no big deal."

"But y'all are going to the same place. . . ." Cade's confusion was endearing, but I sort of wanted to kick him in the shins.

"Yeah, but—"

"Bliss," Garrick interrupted. God, I would never get tired of hearing him say my name in his delicious accent. "It's fine. Really. I don't mind, and I'll have you home in no time. I promise."

He was looking at me like this was the most casual thing in the world. Like having my arms wrapped around him as he drove would be totally okay. Like I didn't still have a bandage on my leg from the last time I'd been on that bike.

Cade yawned. He looked as tired as I felt. I knew if I pushed the issue and wanted to wait for Kelsey, he would wait with me.

I rubbed at my eyes and took a deep breath.

It wasn't deep enough.

"Okay, fine. Thanks . . . Mr. Taylor. And I'll see you tomorrow, Cade."

Cade smiled, oblivious to my torment, and said, "Great!"

He placed a quick kiss on my forehead, said good-night to us both, and then jogged across the road and onto campus.

I didn't even bother with the calming breath this time. I knew it wouldn't help. I set my shoulders and turned to face him.

He watched me for a second, frowning, and then said, "You *cannot* call me Mr. Taylor."

Despite the tension between us, I laughed. It really was ridiculous . . . considering. "Okay . . . Garrick."

There was no good way to do this, so he just handed me

the helmet and climbed on the bike. He didn't have to tell me to be cautious about the exhaust pipe as I got on the bike, but he did anyway.

Tonight he had on a light jacket because a cold front (or, well, as cold as it got in Texas) had just come through. I held on to the jacket instead of him. The ride was even scarier without something more solid to hold on to, but I refused to wrap my arms around him. Mostly because I wasn't sure I would have the willpower to unwrap them if I did.

When we arrived, I was off the bike in seconds. I think I said good-bye. Honestly, I was so panicked that I just bolted. And he let me. When I slipped inside my apartment, I risked a glance back. He was still on the bike, and after a second he started it back up and took off. I watched him go, battling crazy urges to follow him.

No matter what I was feeling . . . there couldn't be anything between us.

On Wednesday I waited in the greenroom until the very last minute so that the class would already be full by the time I got there. I had my headshot and résumé with me as assigned, and I took a seat with Cade way off to the side so that there were about a dozen people between Garrick and me.

About a minute after nine, Garrick called the class to order.

"All right then. Like I said Monday, we're not wasting any time. We're jumping into the thick of things. Today you're doing mock auditions using cold readings from *A Streetcar Named Desire* by Tennessee Williams. If you haven't read it, you should be questioning your major right about now. I've split you into pairs. Those assignments, along with the side you'll be reading, are on the table to my left. I'll send you outside, and you'll have ten minutes to prepare before I call in the first group. You'll note that the scene I've chosen from the play is the scene leading up to the climactic moment when Stanley rapes Blanche, his wife's sister."

"Dude, he rapes her?" That was Dom, obviously one of the ones who should have been reconsidering his major.

"Yes, Dom. Now, the difficulty of auditions is that you often must depict climactic scenes without the benefit of having had an entire performance to build to that point. You're going into this emotionally blind. The moments before you audition are extremely important. You have ten minutes to find a connection with your partner and with your character. Good luck!"

He stepped to the side, and it was like Black Friday at Walmart as actors rushed the table, trying to grab a side and find out who their partner was. I wasn't really feeling up to jumping into the mob, but Kelsey grabbed me by the elbow and didn't give me much choice.

I grabbed the side, recognizing the scene. Garrick wasn't kidding about starting right at the climax. Blanche was pretty much bat-shit crazy already. I glanced at the assignment sheet and wouldn't you know it . . . I was paired with Dom.

I pressed a hand to my forehead, a dull throbbing beginning just over my left eye. Dom swung an arm over my shoulder a moment later.

"What do you know, *Blissful,* we're together again."

I shrugged off his arm and headed toward the door. "Let's get this over with, Dominic."

When I exited the theatre, pairs were already camped out in various places throughout the hallway. The only spot left was directly in front of the theatre doors, which was almost guaranteed to make us the first group picked. That meant we'd have less preparation than everyone else. The thought made me feel like I was going to break out into hives, but clearly the world was against me today. Whatever, at least I'd be done with class early.

"All right, Dom, let's see what we've got."

I spent most of the ten minutes explaining the play and the scene to Dom. He was one of those guys who had a good look and was pretty good at playing the overconfident douche bag (mainly because he *was* an overconfident douche bag), but that was about it.

"So, my guy is drunk, right?"

"Yes, Dom."

"Sweet. And you're crazy?"

I sighed. "Well, sort of. I'm a little delusional, and you destroy those delusions."

"Great. Then I attack you."

I rolled my eyes. What was the point?

"Yes, sure. Anyway, I'm going to open sitting in the chair, and you'll enter from stage left, okay? I can't imagine him making us do the whole scene, because it's kind of long."

And that was all we had time for, because the door opened and Garrick's eyes fell on me. "Bliss, Dom, you ready?"

Dom pulled me to my feet against my will and said, "Sure thing, Garrick."

Ready was the exact opposite of how I felt. I *hated* being unprepared.

Garrick took our headshots and résumés and looked them over in silence for about a minute. I grabbed a chair and moved it to the center of the room and took a seat. I folded my audition side so that the paper wasn't too big and unwieldy. He had us introduce ourselves as if we'd never met him, and then he gave us permission to begin.

The scene opened with Blanche dressed in all her finest clothes, including a tiara, talking to imaginary suitors at an imaginary party.

It took me a few seconds to get into the scene because my own feelings of dread and unease were so contrary to Blanche's blissful ignorance. But once I got there, it was easy to block out the room around me and lose myself in her laughter and her dreams and her delusions. When Dom swaggered into the space, I had to admit, he made a great Stanley. Despite knowing absolutely nothing about the play, he exuded Stanley's charisma, his absolute disregard for Blanche.

I used my unease about the situation with Garrick, letting it seep in and directing it toward Dom. After another half a page, Garrick stopped us.

"Good, good. Bliss, you started a little unsure, but you were dead on by the end. Dom, I think you've got a really good grasp on Stanley." I resisted the urge to roll my eyes. "But . . . I'm not feeling as much connection on your side as I am with Bliss. She's aware of you at all times, adjusting her movements to your movements. I need to see you reacting a little bit more. Let's skip forward to right before you re-enter from the bathroom. Start with Blanche calling Western Union, and let's see if we can't really concentrate on connecting with each other."

I nodded, moving to the opposite side of the space where I had planned to put the imaginary telephone. He'd chosen possibly the hardest part for me to start at. We skipped right over the part where Stanley tore down the nice perfect world I'd dreamed for myself, and I had to convey the same fear and paranoia anyway.

I closed my eyes and took a deep breath.

Fear. Paranoia. How I would feel if someone found out about Garrick and me. Or if he found out I was a virgin. Hell . . . how I felt right before I stopped us from having sex. That was fear and paranoia at its finest.

Feeling a little more confident, I opened my eyes and pantomimed grabbing the telephone. Since I still had to hold my script, I had to forgo pantomiming the earpiece and just pretend to talk into the receiver. I gasped into the phone, asking for an operator.

The fear felt so real that tears pressed at my eyes without any effort on my part. I babbled on, panic rising up and choking my words.

My voice broke over my calls for help. The feeling of being trapped came too easily. It was suffocating.

I heard Dom walk up behind me, and I froze. I backed away, and he stepped between the imaginary door and me. He leered at me, and I didn't have to pretend the revulsion I felt.

I tried to leave, and he stepped in my way. I asked him to let me pass, but he stayed put. Laughing, he started slinking toward me, and I felt the thump of my heart jump slightly.

I slipped out of character just long enough to think that

we were doing a really good job. Far better than I had thought we would. Then Dom's grinning face entered my vision and I was right back in it.

I tried to flee from him, but he kept coming, still laughing. Then his hands closed around my forearms, pulling me up and against him.

I fought, contorting my whole body to try to pull away.

He pulled me against him, squeezing harder, hard enough that it actually hurt, and a little shiver of unease trailed up my spine.

His face was right up against mine, so that I felt the heat of his breath against my face. I was supposed to crumble, defeated, and he would take me offstage for the rape scene, but that's not how things actually went.

Dom dropped his script, gripped my neck, and pulled me forward into a kiss.

Shocked, I pushed against him with my free hand, but he kept going, not realizing that it was *me* protesting, not Blanche. I pushed and writhed, but he was too strong, and his lips were pressed against mine so hard that I couldn't say anything to make him stop. I was gearing up for my final move of protest, a swift knee to the junk, when Dom was ripped off of me.

I gulped in air and saw Garrick, who was seething, release one of Dom's arms that he'd had twisted back at an odd angle.

"Where exactly in this script did you see that particular stage direction, Dominic?" Garrick asked, his tone deadly quiet.

I wasn't wasting time with the logical questions. I flew at Dom, shoving him backward.

"What the hell was that, Dom? The rape scene occurs *offstage,* you asshole!"

He grabbed my wrists as I went to push him again.

"Hey, I was trying to *connect.* I was improvising. That's what actors do!"

Garrick's hand came down on Dom's arm, and he squeezed a little harder than was probably appropriate. Dom let go of my wrists immediately, and I backed away.

"Be that as it may," Garrick began, "actors also respect each other. Unless you'd like to be accused of assault, you okay something like that with your partner beforehand." I could see Garrick's calm facade cracking. "Now go. You're dismissed."

I could tell Dom was pissed. He gave me a scathing look and pushed open the door so hard that it banged against the wall outside. I just could not catch a break this week. Was the world dropping shit on everyone else or just me?

There was a featherlight touch on my arm, and then Garrick was in front of me, cradling my arm in his hands. A bruise was already forming where Dom had grabbed me during the scene. Garrick ran a hand over his face and then looked at me. He said, "I probably could have handled that better."

I didn't realize how much my head was still pounding until I laughed, and the movement sent pain ricocheting through my head. I closed my eyes on instinct. Garrick's fingers brushed along my jaw, sending an earthquake of shivers across my skin from where we touched. I kept my eyes closed, because as long as they were closed, I wasn't doing anything wrong, right? But if I opened them, and I looked at his gorgeous face, and I saw those lips, I'd be crossing into a completely different territory that was most definitely wrong, wrong, wrong.

A whispered "Bliss . . ." was all the warning I had before his lips were on mine.

11

thought of how bad an idea the kiss was for exactly three
seconds before I stopped thinking altogether. His tongue
swept into my mouth, searching and furious and demand-
ing. It was passion in its rawest form. I'd always pretended
to understand chemistry when directors talked about actors
having it together onstage, but now I got it. Whatever happened when he touched me was like a chemical reaction—
molecules changing, shifting, giving off heat.

God, there was so much heat.

Loud laughter that I recognized as Kelsey's sliced through
the haze in my mind, and I tore myself away from Garrick.
There were other students outside waiting to come in. How
long had I been in here alone with him?

He took a step forward to follow me, and I held up a hand.

"Stop! Stop it! You can't just do that! We said we were forgetting about it! *You* said that actually! You can't say that and then do this!"

"I'm sorry."

He didn't look sorry. He looked like he wanted to do it again.

I shook my head and shifted toward the door.

"Wait, Bliss, I am sorry. It won't happen again, okay?"

"Okay." That's what I said, but this felt anything besides okay. He acted like I didn't want that kiss as badly as he did, but hello! He had just as much to lose here as I did! Why was I the only one thinking about the consequences?

I exited to hear Dom mouthing off to a couple of the guys who had gathered close to the doors.

"The guy's a complete dick. He acted like I was trying to rape her or something. It was just a kiss. Not like we haven't done that before."

I rolled my eyes. "And somehow it was even worse this time than it was before. Aren't you supposed to get better with time, Dom?" His friends were laughing, but I still heard Dom call me a bitch.

I kept walking. I had just enough time to buy the biggest cup of coffee I could find before my next class.

The rest of the week was uneventful, thankfully. Garrick kept his distance, and I had enough going on to keep me distracted. We'd gotten our assignments in Directing, which meant it was time to buckle down and read so that I could find a scene. Friday in Senior Prep we talked about our auditions, and he assigned us some reading about the Actors'

CORA CARMACK

Equity Association. So I spent most of the weekend scanning through every play I owned (and most of Cade's) and reading the most boring breakdown of AEA known to the world.

The next week was sign-ups for our first mainstage audition that term—and the next-to-last one for me ever. If I didn't do well on Friday, I only had one more shot at making another show before graduation. I'd been in the first show of the year, and stage-managed another, but nothing since then. They'd already offered me stage manager of the last show of the year, but I'd been too scared to accept yet, in case I didn't get a role in this. God, it was really starting to hit me. I was about to graduate, and my life was nowhere near where I had thought it would be. When I'd started school three and a half years earlier, I'd thought by now I'd have a plan. I'd thought I'd know positively what I wanted to do and where I was going. And if I was honest, I'd thought I would have met the guy I was going to marry by now. I mean, every married couple I knew met in college, and here I was, only months away from graduation, and the idea of marriage at this point seemed preposterous to me.

It didn't help that Mom's immediate question every time we talked was, "Have you met anyone yet?" I wondered briefly how she'd react if I told her the current state of my love life the next time she asked. Maybe she'd freak. Maybe she'd ask when we planned on getting married—it was hard to tell with Mom sometimes.

How can people decide who they want to spend the rest of their life with at this age? I couldn't even decide what to have for dinner! I couldn't decide if I wanted to be an actor, even though I already had $35,000 in student loans telling me I sure as hell better want to be an actor.

By the end of audition week, the thing with Garrick was starting to feel like the "no big deal" I kept saying it was. I got to class at the very last minute and was usually the first one out of the room. True to his word, he kept it professional in class, which meant we only interacted the bare minimum. I never saw him at Grind again, and I'd been there a lot with my friends.

He was in the auditions, but so was every other theatre faculty member. And not even his presence could dampen my excitement for this show. As an actress, I was always drawn more to classical roles than to contemporary ones (hence the Shakespeare obsession), and we were finally doing a Greek show (well, a translation of a Greek show, anyway). *Phaedra* wouldn't have been my first choice, considering it was all about forbidden love, which was so not what I needed right now. But at the very least, I had a great understanding of my character when I auditioned. Sure, Phaedra was lusting after her stepson, not her professor, but the feelings were the same.

I hadn't wanted a role this badly in a long time.

When it was my turn to enter the theatre to audition, I felt good, confident. I knew my lines. I knew my character. I knew what it was like to want someone you couldn't have. And more than anything, I knew what it was to want and not want something all at the same time. I poured every ounce of lust and fear and doubt and shame into that minute-and-a-half performance. I wrenched myself open in a way I never did in real life, because here I could vent and deal and pretend it wasn't about me as I pretended it was about Phaedra. I was more honest under the heat of those lights than I ever was in the light of day.

Soon, it was over, and I was back in the greenroom, left wondering if it had been enough.

When auditions were over, we all went out to celebrate. They would post callbacks in the morning, and that would be a whole new thing to worry about, but for now it was out of our hands.

We were mostly seniors and juniors, and all together we took up an entire section of Stumble Inn. Even though we were at separate tables, we talked across the room to each other obnoxiously and didn't give a damn how many people we annoyed.

We started the night with shots of tequila, which was a little too eerily close to my night there with Garrick, but I shrugged it off. I was there with friends. It would do me some good to loosen up and have some fun.

I was at a table with Cade and Kelsey, of course. Lindsay was there too, along with Jeremy, a cute sophomore I'd drunkenly made out with last year. He'd sort of tagged along a lot since then, but I was pretty sure he knew nothing was going to happen between us. These days he was starry-eyed for our resident sex-crazed beauty, Kelsey. Then there was Victoria, who could easily have passed for Kelsey and Lindsay's love child. She had Kelsey's boobs (and her sluttiness), but Lindsay's "I hate everyone and everything" attitude. And finishing out the table was Rusty, who was pretty much the king of all things random and hilarious.

Jeremy was the only one too young to drink, but the waiter didn't even bother carding the whole table. She looked at Cade's ID and then just scanned the others. We ordered drinks, food, and then some more drinks.

I was feeling pretty good by the time talk came around to auditions.

It was Rusty who broke the ice. "So . . . how about that incest play?"

I rolled my eyes. "It's not incest, Rusty. They're not related by blood."

"Doesn't matter." He shrugged. "I've got a stepmom, and I would shit my pants if she came on to me."

Kelsey laughed. "That probably has more to do with you being gay."

"I've met your stepmom. She can come on to me anytime," Cade said.

If we had been different kinds of people, Rusty would have gotten pissed, maybe punched Cade in the arm . . . or the face. Instead, they high-fived.

"Seriously, though, how did everyone do?" Rusty asked. "I was crap. I'll be lucky to get soldier number two or the servant."

Kelsey butted in. "I would kill to play Aphrodite. I mean, who else has the boobs for it?"

Victoria raised her hand. "Um, hello? Do your eyes not work?" She gestured at her chest.

"Come on, do you even want Aphrodite?"

"Hell no," Victoria said. "Doesn't mean my boobs don't resent you ignoring them."

Wide-eyed, Jeremy said, "I'd never ignore your boobs."

Everyone laughed. Jeremy generally stayed pretty quiet when we were all out together. I guess it could be difficult to keep up with us considering we'd spent every waking moment with each other for the past four years and he was the newbie to the group.

"What about you, Bliss?" Lindsay asked. "We all know you're wetting yourself just thinking about this."

I might have blushed if my cheeks weren't already flushed from the alcohol.

"I think it went well. I just . . . I really get Phaedra, you know?"

Kelsey burst out laughing, and I kicked her under the table.

Cade smiled at me. "What? Are you lusting after some family member I've never met?"

I pushed at his shoulder, and he laughed, wrapping his arm around me and pulling me close.

"I'm kidding, babe."

"I just . . . I get what it's like to want something but to try and force yourself to really believe that you don't. It doesn't even have to be about love. It's about wanting something you can't have or something you don't think you deserve. Hell, we want the parts that our friends get, even though they're our friends and we should be happy for them. We sit in the audience and think about how we would have done a role. We want what we can't have. It's human nature."

I might have gotten a little carried away. The table was quiet when I finished.

Until Rusty said, "You are clearly not drunk enough!" So we drank some more, and our food arrived, looking greasy and glorious.

"You guys do realize there is one major topic we haven't talked about." Victoria raised an eyebrow and continued. "Professor 'I'm sex incarnate and could probably get you pregnant just by looking at you.'"

Most of the guys around the table (minus Rusty) groaned, while most of the girls (minus me but *plus* Rusty) said different ent versions of "Hell yes!"

Victoria fanned herself. "Seriously, that first day when he spoke, I think his accent alone nearly gave me an orgasm."

I stayed quiet, and Kelsey did too, shooting me a questioning glance.

I could excuse myself and go to the bathroom. Would that seem bizarre? It wasn't like I hadn't had a lot to drink.

"Kelsey, why aren't you backing me up here?" Victoria asked. "Can I just call dibs for as soon as we graduate?"

I tried to keep my face passive.

Kelsey smiled. "Oh yeah, he's cute. But he's a little too prim and proper for me. I like a guy who is a bit more dangerous." She winked at Jeremy, and I'm sure his jaw would have detached if it had dropped any lower.

"What? His motorcycle isn't dangerous enough for you?" Cade asked.

"He has a motorcycle? I didn't know that!" She shot me an accusing look like I was betraying her by not relaying this piece of information.

"What happened with him and Dom?" Lindsay asked me. "Dom is still bitching about how he manhandled him during your audition."

Cade's hand slipped from the back of the booth to around my shoulders, and he gave me a quick squeeze.

"Dom's just a jackass. Mr. Taylor just pulled him off of me, that's all."

Rusty smiled and pointed at Cade and me. "You two are so cute. 'Oh, Mr. Taylor this and Mr. Taylor that.' I think you're the only ones still treating him like a teacher instead of a piece of meat."

I rolled my eyes. I never called him Mr. Taylor to his face, but it just felt weird to talk about him with other people and call him Garrick. I felt like they'd be able to read all my secrets on my face and they'd know exactly how un-teacher-like I considered him.

Maybe I did need that bathroom break after all. I nudged Cade, and he slipped out of the booth and let me go. Every step away from that booth, my anxiety eased. I'd stay gone for a few minutes, then I'd come back and they'd be on a completely different conversation and everything would be fine.

I was walking by the bar when I heard my name.

"Bliss!"

I turned, but didn't see anyone.

"Bliss!"

The voice was closer, and this time when I looked behind the bar, I saw him—Bartender Boy.

I smiled and tried to appear happy to see him. But honestly, I couldn't even remember his name. I had been far too focused on other things that night. As always when I thought of Garrick, my stomach flipped and I had to concentrate on not getting lost in the memories.

When we were across the bar from each other, Bartender

Boy said, "Hey, I hope it's not creepy that I remember your name."

It was. A little.

"I promise not to be creeped out if you'll forgive me for not remembering yours."

His lips pulled down in a frown briefly before he smiled and said, "Brandon."

"Right. Brandon. Of course. I'm sorry. It's been a long week."

"Well, let me make it a little bit better." He pulled out a glass and poured me a shot of tequila. "On the house."

I felt awkward taking the shot alone, but I couldn't very well decline it. So I thanked him, shrugged, and downed it in one gulp.

I laughed, not because anything was funny, but just because it seemed like the thing to do.

"Listen," Brandon started. "I don't mean to come on too strong, but do you want to go out sometime?"

Did I want to go out with him? More importantly, did I want to sleep with him? Despite all the craziness with Garrick, I was still a virgin. And I still wished I wasn't. Here was another opportunity to fix that . . . one that didn't involve breaking school rules and risking expulsion. I looked at him. Kelsey had been right—he was cute. And he was definitely interested.

I tried to imagine what sleeping with him might be like. I tried to imagine the shedding of our clothes, his hands against my skin, his lips against mine. I tried, but every image I conjured was of Garrick doing those things, not Brandon.

Damn, why couldn't I just snap my fingers and not be a virgin anymore? Why did sex have to be involved? And why was it that all I could think about was Garrick but I'd even backed out of sex with him?

Why did my brain absolutely refuse to make sense?

Brandon answered his question for himself. "I'm guessing that's probably a no. It usually is if it takes that long to answer."

I smiled a tight, closed-lipped smile. "Sorry. You seem really nice, but I'm just not that interested . . . right now." Damn, I always did that. I sucked at confrontation, so I always added phrases like "right now."

Brandon nodded. "It's cool. Don't worry about it. I, uh, better get back to work, though."

He didn't wait for my answer before he strode down the length of the bar to help a customer at the far end. Sighing, I made my way to the bathroom, where I splashed some water on my face.

It didn't help the chaos in my brain, but I could feel the alcohol tingling in my stomach, and that at least made me feel okay with the chaos.

I returned to the table, where another two shots were waiting for me, courtesy of Cade, and thankfully the conversation was on to some other gossip that didn't involve Garrick. By the time we'd had the next round, my skin felt like a warm blanket and my throat ached from laughing at things that might or might not have actually been funny. We were all gone enough that our conversation had devolved into fragments, inside jokes, and laughter.

"I am *so* drunk," Rusty said, "that I just want to sit in my car and play my accordion until I'm sober."

My laughter was embarrassingly loud. "You have an accordion?"

"Hell yes, I do. Wanna listen to me play?"

"Of course!"

I left my wallet with Cade, so he could pay for mine. I gave him a sloppy kiss on the cheek as a reward.

"Oh! Me too! Me too!" Kelsey cried. She gave her wallet to Cade too, with a head pat instead of the kiss, and Rusty wrapped an arm around each of us.

"Take notes, boys! The ladies always love a man who can play an instrument!"

Lindsay snorted, "Your instrument doesn't even like girls, Rusty!"

"Doesn't mean *they* don't like *it!*"

I'm sure the volume in the bar lowered by half when we were gone, but I couldn't tell the difference. It was still loud in my head. After a few minutes, the rest of the group joined us outside on the hood of Rusty's car, where he was playing his accordion and singing a song he said was French (but I'm pretty sure was just gibberish).

It didn't really matter to us. After a few minutes, we knew the gibberish enough to sing along. We serenaded the bar's patrons as they meandered to their cars at 2:00 A.M. We sang in English and gibberish. We sang Britney Spears and Madonna and *Phantom of the Opera.* Cade did some ridiculous rap where he rhymed "maybe" with "scabies." And we continued serenading until they were all gone and the owner came out to tell us to get lost.

We were all still too drunk to drive, except for maybe Jeremy, but none of our cars were big enough to fit us all.

So, on a whim, I said, "Let's go to my place. It's about half a mile away, but I'm pretty sure I've got vodka in my freezer."

So with a battle cry of "Vodka!" we were off.

I came to regret that night later, but at the time I just hadn't wanted it to end.

12

Somewhere between the bar and my apartment, I lost my shoes. They were low heels, but they were killing my feet all the same. So I simply bent over and pushed them off.

"Whoa, babe, what are you doing?"

I fell into Cade, giggling. I thought I'd been drunk before, but now that a little time had passed . . . it had really hit me. I was possibly further gone than I'd ever been. "Shoes are stupid. Why do people wear them?"

He laughed. "So they don't step on a nail and get tetanus, that's why."

"Wear. Where. Wear. W's are wwweeird."

He laughed, so I laughed, even though I had no idea what was funny.

"You're adorable. Come here. I'll give you a piggyback ride home to save your feet."

"Yay!"

He squatted, and I leapt onto his back. With my shoes in his hands, we teetered down the road. When we walked into my parking lot, I was singing a made-up song that went something like: "Cade is my hero! Zero to hero!"

"What do you mean zero? I was never a zero!"

"Cade is my best friend! One day we're gonna be on *West End!* His car smells like cheese! I just wanna give him a squeeze!"

Rusty called, "Give him a squeeze in private!"

"And Rusty is a douche! And the wind in my hair smells like whoosh!"

Cade laughed. "Don't you mean 'sounds'?"

"What sounds?"

"Never mind," he chuckled.

I saw my apartment come into view.

"Aw, crap. I forgot my purse."

"I've got it, babe."

"You do? You're the best!"

I gave him a loud, smacking kiss. I'd been aiming for his cheek, but I think it landed somewhere on his neck.

About that time I heard Jeremy shout, "Hey! Mr. T! What's up?"

"There's a wrestler here?" I asked.

"Nah, it's Mr. Taylor."

I squeaked, let go of Cade's shoulder, and leaned back to look for Garrick. In doing so, I threw Cade off balance, and both of us toppled to the ground, him on top of me.

I groaned.

"Shiiiit. Cade weighs a lot. Way more than I thought!" I moaned/sang.

I felt adrift, my world rocking like I was out at sea.

Cade said, "Hey, Mr. Taylor."

"Hello, Cade. You all right?"

"Sure thing." He pushed himself up onto his knees and then stood. When he tried to pick me up too, I got a good look at Garrick staring down at me. His hair was all sexy and his grin so gorgeous.

It wasn't fair that he looked so good.

I groaned and covered my eyes.

"Why does the world hate me?"

They both laughed, but it wasn't funny. *Seriously.* Why did the world *hate* me?

"Come on, babe." Cade tried to pull me up, but my body felt dead.

"I don't think I can stand," I told him. "I feel like a wet noodle."

"Do you now?" Cade's amused face looked away from me, and my eyes drifted shut. "Do you mind, Mr. Taylor?"

The next thing I knew I was in the air and I was flying. I leaned to my left, and there was the side of Garrick's face. It was such a pretty side of a face. My arm was around his shoulder, and together, he and Cade were carrying me. Garrick took hold of me completely while Cade crouched and dug through my purse for my keys.

I laid my head against Garrick's chest.

"You smell so good. Why do you always smell so good?"

Cade laughed. "Oookay. And that's our cue to let the professor go."

I let go of Garrick, and Cade's arm wrapped around my middle.

"Sorry, Mr. Taylor."

"It's not a big deal."

"Listen, she'd be horrified if she knew you saw her like this. I swear she's not normally like this. She's just been really stressed lately for some reason."

"It's fine, Cade. I promise. Goodnight, Bliss."

I perked up and snatched the sleeve of his shirt. "No, stay."

Rusty popped up then, his accordion still in hand. "Yeah, Garrick, stay. Bliss Baby has vodka."

Garrick smirked at me. "I think Bliss Baby has had enough. And thank you for the offer, but there are still some lines I shouldn't cross." His eyes met mine, and I knew he wasn't just talking about the party. That sobered me up a little, not much, but enough to know that I was making a fool of myself.

"You guys be careful. Have fun."

Then he walked away, and Cade helped me inside and onto my couch.

The guys went about raiding my fridge, and Kelsey sat by me on the couch and laid across my lap.

"So, your lover was looking pretty great tonight."

"*Kelsey!* Shut up!"

"What? No one heard me."

I looked around. She was right. The guys were stealing chips out of my pantry. Lindsay and Victoria were pouring vodka into glasses of orange juice. When I was sure no one was paying attention, I looked back at Kelsey.

"He always looks good. I don't know how much longer I can handle this. One day I'm going to spontaneously sexually combust and jump him in the middle of class."

She laughed. "As interesting as that would be, you know it's a *terrible* idea. Besides . . . you've already had him. Apparently he was good enough to make you want him again, but it's not like he's a mystery you're dying to puzzle out. You just need a distraction."

I nodded halfheartedly, even though I was pretty sure nothing could distract me from wanting Garrick. And what Kelsey didn't know was that he *was* still a mystery to me. And God, did I want to play Nancy Drew.

Kelsey's eyes gleamed, and she pushed herself up and off my lap.

"Do you know what game I've never played?" she asked the entire room. "Spin the bottle!"

Victoria looked skeptical. "You've never played spin the bottle? Seriously?"

Kelsey shrugged, then turned to peer at me over her shoulder and winked. "What can I say?" she continued. "I was a late bloomer. By the time these ladies came in . . ." (she gestured to her ginormous boobs) ". . . people had stopped needing a game as an excuse to make out."

Cade raised an eyebrow at her. "And we need an excuse now?"

She hopped off the couch and settled Indian-style on the ground, grabbing a half-full water bottle off the coffee table. "Of course not. But it's the *game* that's exciting."

She grabbed my arm and tugged. I landed on the floor in a heap, laughing hysterically.

"See?" Kelsey said. "Bliss is already having fun. Vic, bring the vodka! We'll make this a little more interesting. This is adult spin the bottle. Which means none of that peck on the lips stuff. I wanna see tongue."

"I swear, Kelsey, you're more of a perv than most guys I know," Lindsay said.

"Thank you! Now, I'm not unreasonable. You can choose to do a peck instead . . . but you have to do a shot as a penalty."

Most of the boys looked relieved. Rusty looked disappointed.

"There are far more girls here than guys," Lindsay pointed out.

Victoria grinned. "Perhaps we should go find Garrick and make him join us."

I blanched. "No! Absolutely not."

"God, Bliss, you're such a prude."

Kelsey sent me a knowing smile. And I definitely needed that distraction. I reached forward and set the bottle spinning.

It landed on Rusty, and I didn't even give him a chance to opt out of the kiss. I leaned across the circle, grabbed his collar, and pulled him toward me. I was drunk enough that the kiss was a little sloppy, but we were all drunk, so what did it matter? I kissed him for several seconds longer before pushing him back down and sliding back to my seat.

Rusty whistled. "Damn, girl. If I weren't 110 percent gay, I would ask you out right now."

I threw my head back and laughed. It felt good to let go.

Rusty went next, and poor Jeremy was the next victim. He grabbed the bottle of vodka and said, "No offense, Rusty, but you're just not my type." He smiled, took a big gulp, and then planted a lightning-fast peck on Rusty's lips.

We oohed like middle schoolers.

A knock sounded on the door, and Kelsey hopped up and skipped down the hall. She returned with ten more people from our department.

"You don't mind, do you?" she asked me. It was just like Kelsey to invite first and get permission later. Way past caring, I shook my head anyway.

"Excellent, take your seats, ladies and gentlemen. It's time for some debauchery."

And there was really no other term for it. In a matter of minutes, I'd seen so many friends making out with friends, regardless of whether they liked each other or drove each other crazy or thought of each other as siblings. For one night we put everything aside and let an Aquafina bottle determine our lives.

The next time the bottle landed on me the spinner was a girl. The guys all booed us when we both chose the penalty shot. But they cheered at our peck anyway. Laughing, I spun the bottle again, and it landed on Cade.

Cade had that cute boy-next-door look, right down to the boyish grin he fixed on me now. I shrugged and crawled toward him. Kneeling before him, I put my hands on his shoulders and leaned in.

The kiss was just like any other kiss at first . . . and then suddenly it wasn't. Cade's hand cradled my head and his other pulled me in at the waist. His lips moved against mine feverishly, desperately, like the world was about to end and this was his last chance at happiness.

The kiss was just hard enough to make warmth uncurl in my stomach, but gentle enough that I felt like I was being worshiped. For a moment, I forgot where I was and who I was with and I just basked in the heat, in the pleasure.

Then someone whistled and, piece by piece, the world came back to me. I opened my eyes to stare at my friend, who had kissed me like he wanted to be anything but.

I returned to my side of the circle, ignoring my friends' commentary on the kiss. Dazed and way beyond confused, I retreated into myself through the next few turns.

I could feel eyes on me. Cade's for sure, probably Kelsey's too. But my mind was focused on holding it together, because I was one crack away from disintegrating.

We were drunk. It probably didn't mean anything. And I was so messed up over Garrick that I was desperate for contact with anyone. That was it.

It didn't mean anything.

We're still friends. Cade and I will always be friends.

I stayed for a few more minutes, until my head was spinning too much for me to ignore. I was feeling a bit sick to my stomach.

I stood and excused myself, telling everyone to stay as long as they liked. I told them where to find extra blankets and pillows if they wanted to stay and crash, and then I retreated into my bedroom, crawling under the covers, and dropping the forced smile.

I told myself things would be better in the morning.

13

When morning came, Kelsey was passed out beside me in bed, and there were five people in my living room and one in my bathtub. I smiled at that for half a second before my hangover not so gently reminded me how much I hated the world.

I brushed my teeth and splashed my face with water before returning to my room. When I heard my front door open and close quietly, I peeked my head out of the curtain to see who it was.

Cade had returned with enough greasy breakfast to feed us all.

I took a deep breath and entered the room.

"You are a life-saver!" I whispered.

He looked up, smiling, and handed me a massive bacon, egg, and cheese burrito.

"How are you feeling?"

I frowned. "Like I got hit by a bus. A really heavy one, full of sumo wrestlers."

I hopped up on the counter and regretted it for another ten seconds as my head spun. He took a seat on the bar stool below me.

The burrito was perfect. Thick, fluffy tortilla, hot eggs, delicious salsa.

"I am in love with this burrito. I would marry it if I didn't want to eat it so badly."

"The tragedy of true love," Cade whispered.

I sort of smiled and he sort of smiled, and for the first time in years I felt awkward with Cade. I looked away and focused on the people littered around my living room.

"How was everything after I went to bed?"

"More of the same. If he wasn't already, Jeremy's most definitely head over heels for Kelsey. Victoria left half a pack of cigarette butts on the ground outside. And Rusty was atrociously sick in your bathroom."

I wrinkled my nose.

"Don't worry. It's all cleaned up. I knew you'd have a heart attack if you woke up to that."

I swallowed and a weight settled deep in my stomach.

"You're too good to me, Cade."

He just shrugged. He'd always been too good to me.

"Listen," I started, "about last night . . ."

He scratched at the back of his head, and his mouth pulled up in a halfhearted smile.

"Yeah, I guess we should talk about that, huh?"

His hands settled onto the counter beside me, like he needed to brace himself for what was coming. I cleared my throat, but it didn't make it any easier to talk. "So . . . you?"

His hands tightened until his knuckles turned white. Then, all at once, he let go and answered, "Yeah, I do. I have . . . for a while."

I looked up, but his face was unreadable.

"Why didn't you ever say anything?"

"Because . . . I was scared. You're my best friend. And you almost never date . . . I just didn't think you'd be interested."

Was I interested? I could feel nonsensical tears pressing at the corner of my eyes, and I blinked them away. Cade was a great guy. And I loved spending time with him. And the kiss had definitely been good. It made sense to like him. I wanted to like him, but . . . Garrick was the *but*. Could I stop thinking about Garrick? Stop wanting him?

I heard Cade sigh. "You're not interested, are you?"

God, did his eyes have to be so expressive? I could read every disappointment, every insecurity in them. I loved him; that much was for sure. And I think I could one day be *in love* with him, but I had to get rid of my feelings for Garrick first. If this had happened last semester, would I even be torn?

"Honestly, Cade? I don't know. Is 'maybe' a terrible answer?"

He thought about it for the moment, and I couldn't take the silence.

"It's not that I don't like you. I think you're pretty perfect actually. I just . . . you're my best friend too, and I'm not *sure*. I need to be sure."

"I want you to be sure too." He took a deep breath and smiled. It was a good smile, but not as bright as I was used to from him. "I can live with maybe."

When I arrived at the theatre Monday morning, the callback list had already been posted.

Cast and callback lists are just simple pieces of paper on a wall, but surround them with people who already know your fate and approaching them becomes like walking to the gallows. Eyes turned toward me. I struggled to gauge their reactions. Were they looking at me with pity? Were they just concealing their excitement? Two feet apart, and I existed in an entirely different world from them, from everyone who'd already read that slip of paper. And when I joined them, the pressure wouldn't stop. At the list, you couldn't show emotion. You couldn't cry over a part that wasn't yours or bitch over whose part it had become instead. You couldn't scream in either excitement or rage. You just had to read it and not emote at all. Which might not seem that difficult, except that we were actors. Emoting was what we did.

Cade met me a few feet away.

"Have you already looked?"

He shook his head. "No, I was waiting for you."

Things were still awkward from when we'd talked the day before. We hadn't quite figured out what that all-important "maybe" meant for us. But at that moment it didn't matter. We were two actors about to face rejection or another battle.

We were full to the brim with anxiety, even if we tried not to show it, and there wasn't any room for the multitude of other emotions we had going on between us at that moment.

He took my hand, and I didn't let myself worry about what that could mean. I needed the comfort. I needed him to balance me. And I was fairly certain he needed the same.

We took the last few steps toward the list quickly, and the crowd there adjusted to let us through.

Hippolytus, the stepson, was first on the list. There were seven boys called back, Cade and Jeremy among them.

I looked up at him, and he was completely stoic. Not a thing showed on his face. Not excitement, not nerves. Seven meant the director wasn't sure. It meant he hadn't seen what he wanted yet. It meant that the part was anyone's game, that it would go to whoever stepped it up the most during callbacks.

I squeezed Cade's hand, and immediately he squeezed back.

I know that people talk about their hearts racing all the time and that it doesn't even seem like that big of a deal. But as I looked back at the list, my heart was racing like my whole life rested on that finish line. Sounds were fuzzy in my ears, and my vision had narrowed, and I felt like I was on the verge, on the edge of something terrifying and glorious that could mean flying or falling—success or disaster.

My eyes found the bolded **PHAEDRA** right below **HIP-POLYTUS**.

And then I saw my name, I saw nothing but my own name, like it was the light at the end of the tunnel. It was better than crossing any finish line. It was like taking that first breath of air when I'd felt certain I was drowning, certain I was dying. I stifled the relief and the joy because people were watching and because this was only a callback list. It only meant they hadn't ruled me out yet.

Cade's other hand joined our already linked ones, covering mine completely.

My eyes kept scanning down.

THESEUS.

That couldn't be right. Theseus was a character. My eyes went back up, searching for what I'd missed. There were the seven names under **HIPPOLYTUS.** And there, under **PHAEDRA,** there was only mine.

They weren't calling anyone back.

It was just me.

I'd gotten the part.

And then, breaking all the rules of the list, I screamed. Cade laughed and picked me up at the waist, spinning me around. People around us were clapping, and I knew, based on the way they were looking at us, that some had heard rumors of our kiss. But for a moment, for one blissful moment, none of that mattered.

I'd gotten the part.

14

I went to Senior Prep in a daze.

They always called people back. Even if they were pretty sure they knew who they wanted, it was a chance to be certain, to see the best one more time.

But they cast me outright, which meant they were already certain.

Something swelled in my chest, and before I could help it there were tears building in my eyes. I took a second to myself behind the curtains before entering the space for class.

I tried deep breaths, but that didn't release any of the pent-up emotion in my chest. So I did the next most logical thing.

I danced.

I danced without music. I screamed without sound. I celebrated in silence, in the dark, behind the curtains where no one could see.

Except as my luck would have it, someone totally saw.

"I'm guessing you saw the list."

I froze, my butt still cocked to the left from my last celebratory hip swing. Slowly, I righted my posture, and turned as I said, "Hi, Garrick."

His lips were pursed and his eyes wide, and I knew he was working hard not to laugh. "Hello, Bliss. Congratulations."

My hair was everywhere due to the aforementioned dancing, so I tucked it behind my ears as best I could. "Thank you. I'm, uh, pretty excited."

"As you should be. Your audition . . ." He stepped closer, and as always, his presence stripped away the embarrassment and any other emotion and replaced it with heat, with desire. ". . . Your audition was fantastic. There was no competition."

I swallowed, but the lump in my throat remained. My "thank you" came out as a whisper.

"But Friday night . . ."

"Oh God—"

"As ridiculously cute as you were, please don't get that drunk again. Eric will need you to be at your absolute best for this role."

"Of course," I nodded, petrified. "Absolutely. I promise."

"And . . . I was worried about you too."

"Oh."

His eyes flicked around my face, darting from my no-doubt crazy hair to my eyes to my lips, then quickly down to my leg, where the burn had healed and left a dark pink scar. "I don't like being worried about you."

My heart felt like it was going to make a jailbreak from my rib cage if I didn't do something soon. This was dangerous territory. There were things rearing up inside me, things beyond attraction, beyond an obsession with his looks and his body and his accent—dangerous things. His fingers touched a curl near my cheek, and the proximity of his skin made me feel like I was on the verge of explosion.

I smiled and tried to lighten the situation. "You should probably worry about yourself. Calling me 'cute' again is bound to get you injured, possibly maimed for life."

He took a step closer to me, and the world felt like it was shrinking around the two of us. The hand in my hair swayed closer, his knuckles brushing my cheek. He lowered his voice and said, "Since I can't very well call you the alternative here, 'cute' will have to do for now." My mind flashed back to the first time he'd called me ridiculously "cute." I'd had my panties trapped around my knees. Calling me "ridiculously sexy," he'd then helped me take them off.

Clearly, I needed to learn to stop saying the first thing that popped into my mind. But I couldn't think about that at this moment because my mind was stuck on his last two words . . . *for now, for now, for now.*

He cleared his throat and stepped back, dropping the curl he'd had trapped between his fingers. "Why don't you go take a seat for class?"

I nodded, slipping past him and through the curtains.

There was a seat saved for me between Kelsey and Cade,

both of whom were wearing identically huge grins. I smiled, shaking off the encounter with Garrick to bask once more in my joy. Kelsey leaned in to hug me when I took my seat and whispered in my ear, "I guess being hot for teacher really did help you get into character. I'm so proud of you, honey."

I glared halfheartedly, but nodded my thanks. And then turned to Cade.

We'd held hands earlier, and hugged when I found out about the part, but I wasn't sure what the protocol was now. Living in the world of maybe was . . . complicated.

Before, Cade and I were effortless. Being with him was just as low-pressure as being alone. And now suddenly there was this intensity to everything we did and everything we said. Like my life had been italicized.

When we were touching, I noticed. When we *weren't* touching, I noticed. And suddenly I could find no in between. No maybe.

So I froze.

We were both waiting, stuck in that area between action and refusal. We were nothing. We were inaction. Then Garrick called the class to order, and the awkwardness was postponed for a bit longer.

I knew we'd eventually have to get over this, figure out some way to coexist again. You can postpone only so long before shit hits the fan. But surely I could wait a *little* longer. Today was an exciting day . . . no reason to rain on my own parade.

When class ended, Eric was waiting for me outside.

"Good morning, Bliss. Can I speak to you for a moment?"

I blinked, caught off guard.

"Of course."

He opened the theatre door and gestured for me to re-enter. I followed him through the curtains, and he waved me toward a seat directly beside Garrick. I perched on the seat carefully and glanced between them, unsure of what was happening. Then it dawned on me.

He'd found out.

Why else would he want to speak to Garrick and me?

Oh, my God. What was going to happen to me?

Would they kick me out of the department? Out of the school? At the very least, I'd probably lose my scholarship. How would I pay tuition then?

There was a roaring in my ears, and the pull of gravity felt so heavy that I felt like I would sink right through the floor. Garrick would probably lose his job. What would he do then? He'd go back to Philadelphia or London or somewhere and I'd never see him again.

I turned to him, trying to convey my remorse with a look, but he was . . . smiling?

"Bliss," Eric said, "I have to admit I'm surprised."

Air left my lungs in a rush. "S-sir, I'm so—"

"You've certainly done well in your time here over the past few years, but I had no idea you were capable of the kind of performance you gave in auditions."

I was still clenching my teeth and holding my breath against the coming shame, so it took me a moment to realize it wasn't coming after all.

"You've always been a bit too in your head, I suppose. Controlled. Careful. Mechanical, might be the best word for it. But in those auditions, you were living in the moment. You were feeling instead of thinking. I saw shades of emotion in you—strength and vulnerability, desire and disgust, hope and shame—that were quite simply captivating. I don't know what you're doing or what you've done, but please do continue. You're much better when you make bold choices."

Unbidden, my eyes locked with Garrick's. Did he know? Had he guessed that it was him? That this *thing* between us had me feeling things I'd never felt and taking risks I would have balked at not long ago? My night with him was possibly the only impulsive thing I'd ever done.

"Thank you, sir."

"You're quite welcome. I'm very much looking forward to working with you. Speaking of which, I'd like you to come to callbacks on Wednesday. We'd like you to read some scenes with Hippolytus so that we can get a good idea of chemistry and look onstage."

"Of course, I'll be there."

"Great, Garrick will be there as well to answer any questions for you. He's going to be assistant-directing this production, so if you need anything, you can come to either of us."

He patted me lightly on the shoulder and took off. Then I was alone with Garrick. My heart was still thudding impatiently, either because of the fear that we'd been caught or just because I was sitting beside the one guy I wanted but couldn't have.

"I can't remember if I mentioned it, but I'm really proud of you," Garrick said.

"Thank you. I think I'm still in shock." I was still in shock from *all* of this.

"Well, get used to it. From what I've seen, I don't think you'd have to worry about stage managing unless you just wanted to. You're an actor, Bliss, whether you believe it or not."

I nodded, filing that thought away.

"Have you thought more about that? What you'd like to do after graduation?"

I picked at the frayed threads on the knee of my jeans.

"Not really. . . ."

"Well, if you want to talk about it, you know you can always come to me."

I raised an eyebrow at him, unable to quite put into words how preposterous that idea was.

He said, "I'm serious. You act like we couldn't possibly be friends."

If possible, my eyebrow arched even more. The thought of being friends with him . . . it was beyond imagining. I didn't think about how my friends looked naked. I didn't beat myself up over not sleeping with friends.

He laughed under his breath and shook his head. "Okay, okay. So maybe friends is jumping the gun, but I do hope you'll come to me if you need anything . . . anything at all."

The undercurrent of yearning I felt for him then was different from any of the other pulls toward him I'd felt before. The desire to be with him was still there, but now I wanted more than that. I wanted to curl up in his arms just to rest my head, just to feel his comfort.

Heaven help me, but I wanted my professor to be my boyfriend.

15

Eric was shuffling through papers, searching for something, when I entered the auditorium on Wednesday. "Oh, Bliss, you're early as always. That's great. I seem to be missing my notes, so I'm going to run back upstairs to my office. Take a seat with Garrick and just relax for a moment."

Despite the fact that I already had a part, I was a nervous wreck for these callbacks. What if everyone expected me to be perfect? What if my audition was totally a fluke? I watched Eric leave through the backstage door and wondered: what if he changed his mind?

I took a seat on the row below Garrick, wishing I'd gone and killed some time in the greenroom with the actors waiting and prepping for their second round of auditions. When he leaned down toward me, I said, "Hey . . . *friend.*"

I'd given up trying not to be awkward and was just embracing it instead.

He laughed, which I guess was good. It certainly could have been worse. He said, "Not quite believable, but A for effort."

"Someone's an easy grader."

"Someone just has a soft spot where you are concerned." He was leaning down toward me and even though his face was a good foot away from me, I swear I felt those words like he'd whispered them into my ear. "Sorry," he replied almost immediately. "Sometimes I just forget."

I said, "Me too." But that was a lie. I never really forgot. I wanted to. I wished that I could forget about the miles separating us and just let myself be there, only a foot away, but I couldn't. He cleared his throat, and this time I wasn't imagining his closeness, he was inches from my ear.

"I have to ask you something."

"Okay" came my breathy reply.

"Cade."

I turned, confused, and immediately leaned back because I'd brought our faces too close together.

"That's not a question."

"You're still with him?"

"*With* him?"

"I just—I can't tell. You still sit together in class, but it's different now. So I thought maybe you two had broken it off."

He thought Cade and I were dating? How freaking oblivious was I? The whole world apparently noticed my best friend's feelings for me. So much for being like Nancy Drew—I was clearly the Shaggy and Scooby Doo of this scenario.

"There was nothing to break off," I told him.

"What?"

"Yes! Cade and I aren't together. We never have been." His eyes were wide, and his head tilted in that way that said he didn't believe me. "Is that what you've thought this whole time? That I cheated on him with you?"

Oh, my God. The guy I might or might not have been falling for thought I was a slut. Could things *be* any more screwed up?

His head was shaking back and forth, but I wasn't sure if that was a "no" or just him trying to puzzle this out. "I don't know what I thought. You're always together, and he touches you, he's *always* touching you. Believe me, I've noticed. I'd just assumed that was why . . . well, why you ran out that night."

"I didn't run out because of *Cade.* I had to get my cat . . ."

"Bliss, I'm not an idiot."

God, this was it. Somehow I thought I'd gotten away with that horrible excuse. I mean, obviously, it hadn't completely put him off like I'd originally thought. But he'd always known it was an excuse, he just had the reason wrong. And I couldn't let him know the real reason, not now, not here in this theatre where we were supposed to be professional (though I'm fairly certain professional had already been kicked to the curb).

"I have a cat! I do!" (Damn it . . . why couldn't I ever remember my imaginary cat's gender?) "Um . . . she's gray and adorable and her name is . . ." (I said the first thing that popped into my head) ". . . Hamlet."

I was a genius. I couldn't even invent a girl cat with a girl name. It's like there was this bridge in my brain between the rational and the absurd, and somehow I had burned it.

"You have a cat named Hamlet?"

"I do." Kill me now. "I definitely, definitely do."

That was it. I was going to have to get a cat.

"Fine. So, if you're not dating Cade, what's going on between the two of you?"

I could feel heat leeching into the skin of my neck. "Nothing."

"You are a terrible liar."

I *was* a terrible liar. My ears probably looked like I'd spent an hour in a tanning bed. "It's nothing. It's just something that happened Friday when I was . . . how do you British people say it? Pissed? Sloshed?"

He sat back away from me, but left his hands clenched on the back of my seat. "Did you sleep with him?"

"What? No!"

He didn't lean back toward me, but his grip on the chair loosened. One of his knuckles brushed against my arm. "Good."

"Garrick . . ." He was going to that place we weren't supposed to go.

He smiled cheekily. "What? Just because I can't have you right now, doesn't mean I'm okay with him having you."

My brain tripped over that *right now* phrase again, but I forced my thoughts away from it. "I'm going to pretend you didn't just refer to me like property to be owned."

"Can't we own each other?"

If brains could have orgasms, I'm pretty sure this was

what it would feel like. I shouldn't have liked it, but there was possessiveness in his words that was echoed in his dark eyes, and it sent shivers down my spine until my fingers felt numb with their emptiness. I couldn't answer his question, so I asked my own. "What has gotten into you? I thought you promised me we wouldn't do this again."

He pulled his hands through his hair, his curls sticking out in adorable ways that made my stomach flip-flop.

"I don't know. I just . . . I've been going crazy thinking about the two of you together."

"We kissed. Nothing else."

He flinched back like I'd said Cade and I were getting married and having a houseful of children. I couldn't look at his face. It made me want to do insane things. I repeated myself. "It was just a kiss. It didn't mean anything."

"I don't want anyone else to kiss you."

"Garrick. . . ." I was starting to hate the warning tone in my own voice. If he kept pushing like this, I wouldn't be able to say no much longer. I was going to throw myself at him, most likely just in time for Eric to walk back in.

"I know I'm not being fair. I'm being a right bastard actually. I keep telling myself to leave you alone, but the truth is . . . I'm not sure I can. And now that I know you're not with Cade. . . ."

"What are you saying?"

The backstage door creaked, and I realized how close we were. My heart thrumming like a plucked guitar string, I moved over a few seats seconds before Eric re-entered the space.

He held up his notebook triumphantly. "Got it! And I

brought down a real script for you, Bliss, so you don't have to use the sides."

I fought to calm my heart when Eric handed me the play. Don't look at Garrick. Don't look at him.

It didn't matter . . . I was hyper-aware of him. Even if I moved several rows away from him, I was certain I would know every time he shifted or breathed or looked at me.

The small book felt good in my hands, still warm from Eric's grip, and I had to resist the urge to begin poring over the words that very second to distract me from Garrick. The stage manager, Alyssa, who was a year younger than me, came into the room to announce that we were ready to begin whenever Eric was.

He nodded the go-ahead and then turned to me. "Bliss, we're starting with Hippolytus. I'm going to have them perform their monologues one more time, then I'll have you jump up there. Just stick with what you were doing in your monologue. Play the objective—you want him, but your shame, your fear, is your own obstacle."

I glanced at Garrick. Should be simple enough.

Alyssa came back in, with Jeremy walking calmly in her wake. She took a seat at the tech table, and he stood center stage, his shoulders back, his chin up.

He looked good. I smiled in pride at him. Our little sophomore.

"Hi, Jeremy. I'd like to start by seeing your monologue one more time, just to get things going. Then we'll see how you do with Bliss."

Jeremy cleared his throat. Paused for a moment.

I loved that moment before. It was the height of anticipation and hope. It was like diving off a cliff, knowing that what would come after was terrifying and beautiful and the point of living. That moment . . . it was addicting.

> *I have let myself run on too far.*
> *I see my reason has given way to violence.*

There was desperation in Jeremy's performance as he began, but he sounded young. He looked young. When he spoke, his words and his emotions came rushing out. Like once he'd begun his confession of love for Aricia, there was no stopping the outpouring.

> *My soul, so proud, is finally dependent.*
> *For more than six months, desperate, ashamed,*
> *Bearing throughout the wound with which I'm maimed,*
> *I steeled myself towards you, and myself, in vain. . . .*

I hadn't realized until then that both Hippolytus and Phaedra were in love and ashamed—Phaedra because of whom she loved, and Hippolytus because he loved at all. I could see the shame in Jeremy's performance, eating away at him, and I wondered if that was what I looked like in my audition . . . if that was what I looked like every time I thought of Garrick.

> *Present, I flee you: absent, I find you again.*

Garrick's eyes were on Jeremy, glancing back occasionally at the notes he was writing on the notepad in his lap. That last line was echoing through my head like music, a melody that gets stuck and won't give you any rest.

Present, I fled him. But no matter the distance between us, I kept coming back to him. It all kept coming back to *him*.

Eric stood from his spot and said, "Good. Good. Let's see you with Bliss."

I tore my eyes from Garrick and fumbled for the script. I walked toward the stage, my knees a bit weak and my feet somewhat numb.

As much as I loved Jeremy, it was clear to me within minutes that he was not Hippolytus. For one, he was not the heroic, handsome young man who could turn Phaedra's heart so inside out. He was more of a boy. He had the passion, but sometimes even that wasn't enough.

We moved through two more boys who were also lacking—both lacking in confidence. Those auditions went quickly.

Then it was Cade's turn.

I'd always thought Cade's best asset was his voice. Onstage it took on this low rumble that, no matter the volume, held power. And with a play that was so much about the text and the lyricism in the lines, his voice was perfect. It was always hard to read Eric's face, but he definitely looked happier with Cade than he had during the previous two auditions.

When things fell apart was when Cade and I took the stage together. We were doing the scene where Phaedra first reveals her feelings to Hippolytus. They are speaking of the death of Theseus—Phaedra's husband and Hippolytus's father. Hippolytus has never liked his stepmother. He doesn't know that she has treated him poorly so that she might more easily keep her distance because she loved him even before Theseus supposedly died.

We did fine through the section about Theseus's death, but I was barely halfway through my monologue where I declare my feelings when Eric came out of the house and onto the stage.

"Stop, stop. Cade, what are you doing?"

Cade looked stunned, and maybe on the verge of being sick. "I'm sorry?"

"You despise her. As the revelation of her feelings dawns on you, you should be horrified, disgusted, even angry."

"Of course, sir."

"So then why do you look like a lovesick puppy who returns her affections?"

As if I weren't channeling enough guilt already for this performance, I felt the weight of my own guilt added to it. This was my fault. This wasn't about the play. It was about me. Cade had kept his feelings under wraps for so long, but I'd noticed that, ever since that party, since I'd kissed him, it had all been closer to the surface. He wore his hope like a winter coat layered over the top of all of him.

I didn't look at him as he and Eric spoke because I was not sure I could keep the pity out of my face, and he would hate seeing that. So I looked at Garrick instead. His face was drawn. Even though he was about fifteen feet from me, I felt like I was seeing him from far away. He returned my look for only a moment before his gaze skipped to Cade and his frown deepened. After a few seconds, he met my eyes again and held me there with his stare. There was something different in this look, something changed, something that set my heart beating faster and the hair prickling on the surface of my skin.

Cade and I finished our scene without incident. It wasn't the strongest performance he could have given, but I thought it was still the best so far. Though I was biased, I guess. I should have been happy that my friend had trouble even acting disgusted with me. But in the back of my mind a thought had been planted, its roots digging deeper despite my attempts to push it away.

If he knew the real reason I'd said maybe . . . if he knew what was keeping us apart . . . he probably wouldn't have any trouble despising me.

I was a little unfocused through the next callback. So much so that Eric decided it was time to give me a break. Needing the fresh air, I slipped out the emergency exit (which was never alarmed), and I knew before I heard the door creak open again behind me that Garrick would follow.

"You're doing well," he said.

I blew out a quick breath. It might have been a laugh, if I'd had more energy. "Yeah, that's why you're out here trying to make me feel better."

"My reasons for being out here are entirely selfish."

I kept thinking I would get used to him saying things like that, his directness.

I never did.

"You were right. You *are* acting like a right bastard."

What little heat there was in my words left when he grinned.

He walked around the side of me, staring out at some distant point on the campus. "I keep thinking that this play is a sign. It's so much like us."

"Am I the lust-filled mother in this situation or are you?"

His eyes came back to me, dipping and scanning the curves and lines of my body. "Oh, that's definitely me," he answered. "Phaedra keeps saying she's being selfish. That she hates herself for it, but she does it anyway. She can't deny herself what she wants, even if it brings about her downfall and his."

"And have you learned anything from our literary parallel?"

"Not really. I keep thinking that she would do it all over again if there were a chance . . . a chance that it could go right. Even if ninety-nine times out of a hundred the story ends badly, it's worth it if only once she gets a happy ending."

"Listen, Garrick, while this parallel you're drawing is lovely, especially with that accent, I'm a little tired of the metaphors and of being compared to doomed love stories. Just say what you want to say. I've been puzzling out ancient text all night. I don't want to have to decipher you too."

"I'm saying that I was wrong." He took a step closer, and my exhaustion fled, replaced with electricity under my skin. "I'm saying I like you. I'm saying I don't give a damn that I'm your teacher."

Then he kissed me.

I pushed him back, before my heart and mind got swept away. The pleasure hit me after the kiss was already over, so that it felt like an echo. And even though I was the one who pushed him away, I missed him.

"Garrick, this is crazy."

"I like crazy."

The question was . . . did I? This was the craziest thing

I'd ever done, and it both terrified and excited me. I backed away, needing the distance to think, to wrap my brain around the insanity. There were so many ways for this to go badly. But then again, for the first time ever, I found my own life more interesting than the story of a character on a page. And God, did I want to know the ending.

And hadn't Eric said I was better when I made bold choices? He'd been talking about acting, but didn't it hold true for life too?

Garrick's hand brushed across my forehead, then pushed back into my hair.

"Just think about it."

Oh, I would think about it. It would likely be all I could think about.

He pressed a quick, barely there kiss to my forehead and left me outside, my thoughts in a jumble and my heart a mess.

16

Why in the world would you want a cat?" Kelsey asked as we left Directing the next day.

"I just do, okay? Do you want to come or not?"

She shrugged. "Can't. Sorry. I've got work. Just take Cade."

As if he'd been summoned, Cade popped up between us, and I wondered how long he'd been listening to our conversation.

"Take me where?"

I said, "I'm going to the humane society to get a cat."

"Oh. Cool," he said, nodding. "I wish I weren't living in the dorms. I'd love to have a dog."

I was aware of the careful space he kept between us and the near-continuous bobbing of his head, like the nodding had given him something to do and he didn't want to give it up.

Kelsey pulled her sunglasses down off her head and over her eyes even though we were still indoors. "Well, as fun as this is, I've got to jet. You two have fun at the pound. Don't come home a cat lady, Bliss." Kelsey was oblivious to the panicked look I'd shot her. Cade and I hadn't really been alone since the whole maybe conversation. He switched his messenger bag to his other shoulder, fidgeting like he always did when he was nervous.

"If you want to go alone—it's cool."

"No, no. You should come." We had to get over this. And I saw only two ways—we got together or we didn't. The waiting was going to kill our relationship (it was already pretty maimed). If we had to have this conversation, around cute animals was probably the best place.

"Okay. Cool," he said.

Cool . . . yeah.

I was glad to be the one driving. It gave me a way to occupy my body and my mind. And it was my car, so I could turn the music up as loud as I wanted. What I hadn't counted on was Cade being at home enough in my car to turn it down.

"So, what made you decide to get a cat?"

Oh, you know. I nearly had a one-night stand with our professor, but ran away using my imaginary cat as an excuse, and now he might want us to be *together* together, even though it's the worst idea ever, but I kind of don't care either, because my body and probably my heart are telling me it's the *best* idea ever.

So now I need a cat so he won't realize I was lying about the cat because I'm a virgin and chickened out of having sex with him.

"Just want one" was what I actually answered.

"Oh. Cool."

If he said "cool" one more time, I was going to scream.

I pulled into the humane society parking lot, wishing I had told Cade I wanted to go alone after all.

I needed something fuzzy and adorable in my hands, stat.

We stepped inside to that distinct medicated smell that's reserved for pounds and veterinarians. The lady at the front desk even looked vaguely feline, like working here was in her DNA. Her face was slightly pointed, her eyes tilted, and her hair short and fuzzy.

"Hello there! How can I help you?"

"Hi," I said. "I'm interested in adopting a cat."

She clapped tiny hands that I envisioned as paws. "That's fantastic. We have plenty of great candidates. Why don't I take you back to the cat room and give you two a chance to look around?"

We followed her down the hall, that antiseptic smell growing stronger, no doubt covering the odor of a multitude of animals housed in one place.

"Here we are."

The room was stacked with cages, and I don't know if the chorus of meows began at our entrance or if it was constant, but we were surrounded by sound.

"I'll leave you two alone. All we ask is that you take only one animal out at a time." With a wide Cheshire Cat smile and a wave, she left.

In silence, I peeked into cages, feeling lost.

I liked cats, but I wasn't sure I actually wanted one. What would I do with it when I graduated? Was it worth it for a boy? Was it worth it just to have sex? I mean, it wasn't like there weren't other options for losing my virginity.

I looked at Cade, who had his fingers slipped inside a nearby cage, petting a midnight black cat.

If I was honest, this wasn't just about having sex, even if it had started that way. As much as I wanted Garrick, I was pretty sure that if I tried to sleep with him again, it would turn into a repeat of my first awkward performance.

"You know what?" I said out loud. "Maybe I'm not ready for a cat."

I turned to leave, but Cade stepped in my way.

"Whoa. Wishy-washy much? You haven't even held one. Give it a chance."

He opened the cage with the black cat and pulled it into his arms. He brought it toward me, rubbing at the cat's jaw. Even though I was eye level with the furball, I could hear the engine roar of his purrs.

I took a step back and tried to explain without really explaining. "It's not that I don't like cats. And really, I think I would *enjoy* having . . . a cat. But what if I *get a cat* before I'm ready? What if I choose the wrong cat? Or what if I'm bad at it . . . being a cat owner, I mean?"

God, how much easier would this be if I could say what I was really thinking?

Cade rolled his eyes and pushed the animal into my arms. "Bliss, you couldn't be bad at this if you tried."

I could be bad at sex, though. Knowing my overactive, neurotic brain, I could be completely awful at it.

The cat reached up and rubbed the top of its head against my chin. It *was* pretty adorable. Cade was beaming at me, and I thought, *Maybe Cade would be the better choice.* Would I be so terrified of sex if I were having it with Cade?

The thought made me feel shaky, unsteady.

I passed the cat back into his arms, still unsure, but feeling a little calmer. I came to the line of cages and searched for a gray one that could pass for a Hamlet. When I found her, Fate must have been laughing at me. She was hunkered down in the back of her cage, her large green eyes wary. I pulled the cage door open, and she replied with a guttural growl.

Of course . . . I would get the scary cat.

Over my shoulder, Cade said, "You're not serious."

If only I weren't. But I'd told Garrick that Hamlet was gray.

"Sometimes it's the scary things in life that are the most worthwhile," I told him. I'm pretty sure I'd read that in a fortune cookie once upon a time. That made it wise, right?

I reached my hands into the cage, ready for a bite or a scratch or full-on massacre, but as my hands circled around the middle of the beast she reacted only with a low groan.

Cade shook his head, confused. "Why wouldn't you want this one?" He pulled the black cat up close to his face. "He's so sweet!"

In contrast, the cat in my arms was on full alert—her legs straight, eyes wide. I had a feeling if I tried to hold her any closer, she would maul me. I sat her down on the ground and she took off, hiding beneath a nearby bench.

I knew Cade was only asking about the cat, but I heard another question. One he hadn't asked, not today anyway. And

Cade was sweet, and the thought of being with him didn't leave me immobilized with fear. The thought of being with him didn't leave me with any overpowering emotion actually.

That was when I knew.

"Cade . . . I need to take back my maybe."

I swear even the cats stopped their meowing. I could imagine their stunned silence. I wondered what cat-speak was for *Oh, no, she didn't.*

"Oh."

I wished he would react—scream, argue, anything. I waited for him to lock up like that cat, claws out, teeth bared. Instead, he walked calmly away and placed the black cat carefully in his cage, probably so we wouldn't have more than one cat out at once like the lady said. That was Cade, always thinking about the rules. That's how I'd always been too, but I was starting to think it wasn't how I wanted to be now.

His movement was mechanical, simple, precise. He pulled the cage door closed and turned the latch with a sharp snap. He kept his back to me as he spoke.

"Am I allowed to ask why?"

I breathed out. I owed him that much, but how could I tell him this? He couldn't know. If I was going to do this thing with Garrick (which, who was I kidding? I probably was), then no one could know. Not even my best friends.

"I . . . there might be someone else."

"Might be?"

This was stick-your-hand-into-a-blender terrible. He wouldn't look at me, and the heart in my chest felt paper-thin, like tissue paper, which meant I was pretty damn close to heartless, doing this to my best friend.

"Things are still a little . . . complex. But I like him, a lot. I was going to wait it out, see if the feelings went away, so that maybe you and I could. . ." I trailed off, not wanting to put into words what I'd been thinking. There was no point. "But, Cade, I can't handle how things have been. It's been less than a week, and I feel like I'm dying. I hate questioning everything I do around you, wondering if it's okay, wondering if it crosses a line, wondering if I'm hurting you. I miss my best friend, even when I'm standing right beside you. So . . . I had to make a choice. And I need you in my life too much to screw us up. If I'd told you yes, and then my feelings for him didn't go away . . . I couldn't do that. Please tell me I haven't screwed this up already. Please, please."

He turned then, and I was startled by the hurt I saw in him. Cade's face looked foreign with a frown. "I want to say we're okay, Bliss. I need you too. But I can't pretend I wasn't hoping this would go somewhere. I don't know if I can do it. The truth is . . . you are hurting me. Not on purpose, I know that. But I love you, and every second that you don't love me back . . . it hurts."

"Cade. . ." I reached for him.

"Don't, please. I can't."

The medicated smell of the shelter was suddenly overpowering, nauseating.

I asked, "Can't what? Can't be my friend?"

"I don't know, Bliss. I just don't know. *Maybe.*" The hint of bitterness in his tone was small, but it struck me like a slap across the face anyway. He walked out the door, and I sank down on the bench, feeling frayed and burnt and bruised. My tissue paper heart was shredded.

I sat there, trying to puzzle out how I could have done this better. Was there any possible path I could have taken that wouldn't have fucked this up so completely? Would telling him no straight out have been better? Should I have waited until the year was over and Garrick had left and then tried to have something with Cade?

My mother had told me once when I was little and had a friendship fall apart that some relationships just end. Like a star, they burn bright and brilliant, and then nothing in particular goes wrong, they just reach their end. They burn out.

I couldn't fathom my friendship with Cade being over.

Something nudged at my calf, and then the gray cat's head poked between my legs. She pulled her whole body through the space between my legs, rubbing against me as she went. She circled back and pressed her head against my shin. I reached a hand down, and she froze, flattening against the floor in fear. More slowly, I moved until my hand pressed against her back, sliding along her fur in one smooth stroke. Her body relaxed, and I petted her again.

I eased myself down onto the floor beside her. She locked up again, but she didn't run. When I was certain she was comfortable with me, I picked her up in my arms. I pressed my face against her fur, absorbing the comfort she didn't realize she was giving.

"Let's make a deal, Hamlet. I'll help you be less afraid if you help me too."

17

By the time I had filled out the necessary paperwork and had Hamlet housed inside a cheap cardboard cat carrier, nearly thirty minutes had passed since Cade had walked out to my car. Standing in the parking lot, I couldn't find him anywhere.

I pulled out my phone. No text.

I looked on my windshield. No note.

I called his phone. No answer.

I called his phone again. Straight to voicemail.

By the beep, I was crying.

"Cade, I'm sorry. I'm so sorry. I don't know how to make this better. I just want us to be how we've always been. God, that's stupid. I know we can't be. I know things can't be how they were before, but . . . I don't know. Never mind. Just . . . let me know you're okay. You're not at my car, and I don't know how you got home, if you got home. Just call me. Please. Let's talk about this."

A few minutes later, I was sitting beside my car in the gravel, my jeans smeared with dust, and I got a text.

I'm fine.

I tried to call again. Straight to voicemail again.

And as hard as I tried to feel otherwise, as hard as I tried to hope that we'd get past this, I already felt it. I felt burnt out.

Maybe it was the grief. Maybe I'd just finally gone crazy. Maybe I just didn't have anywhere else to go. But when I got back to my apartment complex, I didn't go to my apartment.

Hamlet in hand, I went to Garrick's.

I don't know what I looked like when he opened the door. I don't really want to know. But he opened the door wider almost instantly, gesturing me in with no questions asked.

I'd never been in his apartment. I should have taken it all in or asked him to show me around. I should have said something, but the only thing on the tip of my tongue was a sob, and it took all of my energy, all of my concentration, to hold that inside.

But even that wasn't enough when his fingers tilted my chin up. He spoke my name, and I saw the worried look in those eyes. The tears streamed out of me like a cup overflowing, and I couldn't control it, couldn't breathe right, couldn't explain.

He took Hamlet's box out of my hands and wrapped an

arm around my shoulder. He led me down a hallway almost identical to mine into a living room that was vastly different. It was filled with books, some on shelves, some in stacks on the floor. The furniture was simple, slightly modern, but not so modern that I hesitated to sink into the cushions of the black couch, snatching up a white pillow to hug to my chest. Then Garrick was beside me, pulling the soft pillow out of my hands and replacing its comfort with himself. He pulled me into his lap, cradling me like a child, wiping away my tears, brushing back my hair, rubbing at my back.

"He hates me," I finally managed. Garrick hadn't asked, but his concern tugged at me anyway, tugged the words right from my mouth.

"Who does?"

Quick, short breaths puttered from my lips, little whimpers that I couldn't seem to control.

"C-Cade."

"Cade could never hate you," he said.

"He does. He left. He won't even talk to me." I dissolved into another fit of tears, and he just pulled me in close, tucking my head underneath his chin, against his chest.

He let me cry, murmuring things all the while. *You'll be okay. Things will work out. Calm down. Breathe, Bliss. I'm here. It will be okay. Whatever it is, we'll take care of it. It's okay.*

He must have whispered a thousand variations. But he never stopped trying, no matter how much I wasn't hearing him. When I was finished crying, I was too tired to do anything else. I lay limply against him, doing nothing but breathing in and breathing out. And he held me still. Finally, a noise broke through the fog. A low, annoyed groan.

Hamlet. I'd left Hamlet trapped in that box this whole time.

Filled with purpose, I sat up, clearheaded again for the moment.

"I'm sorry, I need to take her home." I was standing and reaching for her crate, when Garrick took me by the elbows.

"Stay, love. You're upset. I'll take care of the cat."

No. I couldn't let him do that. Because then he'd see that all the cat stuff I'd bought the night before was still brand-new and unused.

"No, it's okay. I really should go. I'm okay now. Thanks."

"Bliss, please, talk to me."

My body was leaning toward him against my will, aching for his comfort again, but I hadn't made a decision yet.

"I don't know . . ."

"How about this. You go home and take care of the cat, and in a little while I'll bring dinner. We can talk or just watch a movie or whatever you need to do. I just . . . if you leave like this, I'll go crazy worrying about you."

After a moment, I nodded.

"Okay."

"Really?"

"Yes, just give me an hour, okay?"

He smiled, and I knew . . . I was in trouble.

I was pretty sure my new cat hated me.

Not that I blamed her, after I left her in that box for so long.

No matter what I did, she let out that closed-mouth growl every time I took a step anywhere near her. I set up food for her in the kitchen, which she ignored. I made a litter box and put it in a storage closet. I picked her up and carried her to the box, placing her inside so she'd know where it was. She hissed once and then ran, kicking up litter in her wake. She disappeared under my couch, only her glowing, evil eyes visible in the darkness.

Why hadn't I told Garrick I had a cat named Lady Macbeth? That would have been so much more fitting.

For the rest of the time, I was left alone with my thoughts, which were about as pleasant as the Ebola virus. I straightened up the living room, then thought about running away. I straightened up my bedroom, then rushed to the bathroom, certain I was going to vomit. I didn't. I almost wished I had. I could have said I was sick.

Before I really got the chance to talk myself into or out of this, there was a knock at the door.

My heart felt like someone was using it as a trampoline. I took a deep breath. I hadn't promised him anything. He'd said we could talk. Or watch a movie. Or do whatever I wanted. This didn't have to be a big deal.

When I opened the door, Garrick looked so cheerful that it was hard to keep dreading his presence.

"I forgot to ask what you wanted, so I got pizza, a burger, and a salad." He was balancing all three in his hands, and I was all at once overwhelmed with how much I *liked* him. Not just in a romantic way. In general. He was kind of amazing.

I smiled. "Pizza is good."

I moved back, and he stepped inside my apartment. As much as I had been freaking out earlier, it felt natural to have

him here. Not that I wasn't still nervous, it was just . . . he felt
like he belonged.

We made our way into my kitchen/living room, and he set
the food on the small circular island that jutted out from my
kitchen counter. I busied myself getting us drinks and plates,
and when there was nothing else I could distract myself with,
I pulled out one of the bar stools tucked underneath the
island counter and took a seat beside him. I pulled a slice of
pizza onto my plate, and he opened the salad.

I narrowed my eyes at him.

"You are not seriously going to sit there and eat a salad
while I stuff my face with greasy goodness, are you?"

He dumped dressing on top of his lettuce and grinned.
"Oh, I'm going to eat the burger too. And some pizza, if you
leave me any."

I rolled my eyes. Guys sucked.

We talked. Not really about anything that mattered. He
balked when I dipped my pizza in ranch. When I made him
try it, he puckered his face up like it was gross, but I saw him
dip a slice again later when I was up refilling my drink. It
wasn't until I was so full that I felt like I was going to burst
that he brought up my earlier breakdown.

"So, can you tell me now what happened with Cade?"

I picked at the pepperoni on the half-eaten slice of pizza
on my plate.

"We had a fight, I guess. I think. I'm not sure. We've
never really had a fight before."

"About?"

I pushed out the air I'd been holding in my lungs and set

about returning things to the fridge and placing our plates in the sink.

"About the kiss."

I could imagine Garrick's reaction without seeing it, so I decided to go ahead and wash the dishes . . . by hand . . . even though I had a dishwasher.

"He likes me," I continued. "He told me after the kiss, and we've been trying to act like nothing changed, but it was awful, and I just got tired of pretending things were normal."

He appeared beside me, taking a plate and drying it for me. He must have realized by now that it was easier for me to talk when we weren't looking at each other because he kept his eyes focused on the plate long after it was dry.

"So, what did you do?"

"I told him I didn't think it was going to happen."

"You weren't even a little interested?" Garrick asked.

I didn't think Garrick really wanted to hear this, but he was going to get what he asked for. I needed someone to vent to.

"I thought about it. Cade is sweet, and I like being with him, but he doesn't really make me *feel* anything."

He stopped staring at the plate and turned toward me, leaning his hip against the counter beside me.

"Do I make you feel anything?"

I glanced up at him just long enough to see if he was joking. He wasn't. I looked away.

"That's a stupid question."

"Is it? You're harder to read than you think you are."

I dried my hands on a towel and moved to the couch, pushing myself into a corner and dragging a pillow into my lap.

"I'm serious," Garrick continued. "Sometimes you react . . .

like, well, how I want you to react. But then other times, like outside during callbacks, you push me away like you're not affected by me the way I am by you."

I squeezed the pillow tighter to my chest.

"I'm affected, Garrick. I'm just also confused . . . and worried. And I don't understand why you aren't."

He took a seat on the opposite side of the couch, the entire middle cushion separating us.

"I think that's all I do is worry," he said.

"And you still think this is smart?"

He shook his head, laughing. "Oh, it's definitely not smart. I know that. But honestly, Bliss? I'm miserable here. It's great to have a steady job, and I'm enjoying teaching, but I don't have any friends left here. I go to work, and then I go back to my apartment. And I think about you because I can't help it, and there's nothing else to distract me. Especially when I know you are only one building away. The night we met . . . Bliss, I don't normally do things like that. But I was second-guessing everything about coming here, and you were everything I needed. I don't know how many times I've stopped myself from coming over here and knocking on your door. And yes, seeing you with Cade was definitely motivation, but more than that . . . I just like you, Bliss. As a teacher. As a person. As a guy."

It was hard to keep my breathing steady, hard to keep the longing from showing on my face, hard to keep from reaching for him.

"So what now?" I asked him.

"I have absolutely no idea."

I had so many ideas. That was the problem.

"If we do this . . ." I started, and then stopped. His entire posture had changed, and I felt it echoed in my own. We were about to cross a line, and we both knew it. "If we do this, we have to be careful." He nodded, his eyes fixed on me. "And I think we should take it slow. If we get caught up in this too fast, we'll get sloppy." And I needed more time to think about this, about sex with him, about whether it was something I wanted to do.

I wasn't sure slow was something we *could* do, but it was the only way I could do this without freaking out. Who was I kidding? I was going to freak out regardless. The difference was whether it was a "feel like I'm going to be sick" freak-out or a "lock myself in my apartment for a week" freak-out.

"Okay." Garrick slid closer to me on the couch, halfway onto the middle cushion. "I can do careful . . . and slow."

My skin was invaded with goose bumps when he reached a hand out to me. I let myself be afraid for a second, but then the need to touch him overpowered even my fear. I pushed the pillow out of my lap and slid toward him. I put my hand in his, and he pulled it up to his mouth, holding it there against his lips. He closed his eyes, and the simple touch soaked into my body, soothing my anxiety.

Like a key into a lock, my body fell into his, fitting perfectly. With my head on his chest and his arm around my shoulder, I took a deep breath and knew there was no going back.

18

The easiness of the night before had evaporated by Friday morning. Cade wasn't mad per se, but he wasn't much of anything really. He didn't talk to me in the greenroom or sit by me in class. When I joined a conversation, he left it. I was a habit, and he appeared to be quitting cold turkey.

Garrick's gentle smile in Senior Prep helped. We'd commandeered the computers in the design lab for the day to do postgrad research. Some of us were researching graduate schools, others scouring for internships. Kelsey was looking at airline tickets and hostels in random cities around the world.

I was looking at the search engine home page.

Curling his hands around the back of my chair, Garrick leaned his body in close to mine. The proximity was altogether distracting.

"What are you thinking, Bliss?"

I should have said, *You. Naked.* That would have shocked him. Not that I was actually thinking of him naked . . . well, now that I mentioned it I was . . . damn.

Like I said, distracting.

I shook my head because I didn't have an answer, not one I could say out loud. He stepped around me and leaned on the table, looking at me.

"Acting or stage management?" The gaze he fixed on me felt too personal in this room full of my classmates, even if none of them were looking—well, other than Kelsey. She watched pretty much anytime Garrick talked to me, which reminded me that we had to be careful.

"I don't know," I muttered.

"Okay, well, what about a city? You can start looking at apartments. That's certainly something you've got to think about, especially if you're going to New York."

I stared at the search engine box. It was taunting me.

"I can't afford New York," I told him.

"That's okay. Most people can't. There are plenty of regional markets to consider. Philadelphia." I jerked around to face him. Was he telling me to look at Philadelphia? Where he lived? Was he trying to tell me something or was I reading too far into this? His face was blank as he continued. "Dallas and Houston both have a fair amount of work. Chicago. Seattle. Boston. D.C. There's plenty to choose from actually." I turned back toward my computer, my heart still beating a little too fast. I was definitely reading into this. It wasn't like we were serious. We'd spent the evening cuddled on my couch. That didn't mean that we were together or that I was ready to move halfway across the country with him.

"Just explore. Look up something," he said before leaving me to continue walking around the room.

I placed my fingers on the keys, but they felt like lead, too weighted to move. I stared at the key with the letter "P." I could see Kelsey watching me out of the corner of my eye, and as curious as I was now about Philadelphia, I typed "stage management internships" into the search engine.

Then I clicked from web page to web page, watching the clock in the corner of my screen, willing the numbers to change faster.

When class was over, my relief was short-lived.

The cast list had been posted.

I was still Phaedra, which was good. How embarrassing would it have been if Eric had changed his mind? Kelsey got Aphrodite, like she wanted. Rusty *did* get a soldier, just like he'd predicted.

And Cade was Hippolytus.

I knocked on Garrick's door that evening, nervous despite our agreement to take things slow. We hadn't really talked about doing anything tonight, and despite our tenuous relationship, we'd yet to exchange numbers. So I hoped I wasn't being needy by seeking him out a second night in a row. Hamlet definitely was glad to have me out of the apartment. We still weren't coexisting very well.

My worry eased when he opened the door and said, "Oh,

thank God. I've been thinking about coming round to your place for over an hour, but I was afraid I'd knock on the door and you'd have people over or something."

I laughed.

"Maybe we should actually exchange numbers then."

He said, "Are you going to put me in your phone under some secret code name so that no one knows who I am when I text you dirty things?"

My eyes widened. "Are you planning to text me dirty things?"

His eyes danced with amusement, and that blinding grin was back on his face. "I'm not ruling it out."

Oh. *Oh.* My nerves shot back up.

He took my hand and pulled me into his living room where a book was open on his sofa. It was poetry, of course, because he was perfect and woefully out of my league. He marked his page and placed the collection on top of a pile of books at the edge of the sofa.

He reached and laced our fingers together in the space between us. I wanted to lean into him, wrap myself around him, and not move from his arms until I had to, but I still felt awkward. Were we in that place yet where we could just do that? Or did we have to work our way up to it?

"So . . . cast list?" he asked.

I groaned and leaned my head back against his couch.

"It's not that bad, is it?"

"That depends on whether or not Cade is speaking to me by the time rehearsal rolls around in two weeks."

I didn't have to worry about easing into it, because

Garrick had no qualms about pulling me to him. My head fit perfectly onto the curve of his shoulder.

"Cade seems like a reasonable guy. I'm sure after a while to process everything, he'll be better."

I nodded, hoping he was right, but not feeling confident. Cade was reasonable. Trouble was . . . reason probably told him to stay the hell away from me if he didn't want his heart stomped on. And maybe that would be for the best.

He deserved someone better.

"All right," Garrick said. "Enough about that. I don't like that sad look on your face. Unfortunately, our options for the evening are limited, since we can't actually go anywhere. So how about a movie?"

I pulled a smile onto my face. When he smiled back, it took less effort to hold it there. "A movie sounds good."

He picked something funny, probably in an effort to cheer me up. Then he flicked off the lights and joined me again on the couch. As the opening credits began, he leaned back, pulling me with him. He was stretched out on his back, and I was on my side, fitted between him and the back of the couch. I hesitated a moment before laying my head against his chest.

I tried to watch the movie, I really did, but it was hard to concentrate with his steady, even breaths ruffling my hair and his hand tracing up and down my spine. It was somewhere between ticklish and seductive. I was hyper-aware of the way every once in a while his finger would continue a little farther down my back, until he barely touched the stretch of skin between the bottom of my shirt and the top of my shorts. He would stay there for only the barest of seconds before returning up my back. Then his finger danced up to the sensitive skin at the back of my neck, and I had to hold back a moan. I glanced up at him quickly, but he was focused on the movie, completely unaware of the madness he was driving me to.

Finally, I decided it was time for him to get a dose of what I was feeling. I uncurled the fist I had resting on his chest, pressing my fingertips ever so slightly into his chest. I started by tracing the abstract design on his T-shirt, something from a band, I think. But once I'd done that, I kept trailing my hands across his chest, across the curve of one pec, down the sternum to his ridged stomach, back up his chest to the muscles stretching from his shoulder to his bicep. When my hand imitated one of his moves, barely tracing along the hem of his T-shirt, his hand on my back stilled.

Somehow the stillness set me even more on edge.

Feeling a little brave, I went back to the hem, pushing my fingers up and under his shirt, using my fingernails to draw the barest of touches across his skin. The hand on my back moved, sliding up past my neck and into my hair. I flattened my hand, pressing my palm against his warm skin. The hand in my hair tightened, not enough to hurt, but just enough so that he could use it to tilt my head backward slightly.

He gazed at me, no trace of teasing grin, his blue eyes appearing black in the darkened room. His eyes danced around my face, flicking most frequently between my eyes and my lips. The anticipation was killing me, and I dug my fingers into his skin. His breathing wasn't so steady anymore, but he still only looked at me. I licked my lips, and his gaze stayed there longer, so long that heat was pooling between my legs just because of the anticipation alone, and I squirmed, trying to relieve the pressure.

When I lifted one of my legs, curling it around his own, he finally took action.

The hand in my hair pulled me forward, and he met me halfway.

All of the anticipation of the last ten minutes focused into the point where our lips met. The connection was too small to bring to mind fireworks, but it was something close, like the excitement of holding a sparkler—the rush of feeling the sparks creep closer to your hand.

His mouth stayed closed, and even though I'd tasted him several times before, the mystery was killing me.

It felt like a first kiss.

He pulled back and pressed his forehead against mine.

"Thank you," he said.

Thank you? Was that like a "Thanks but no thanks"? "Thanks, but I'm watching a movie, leave me alone"?

"For?"

"For giving this a chance. I know you were . . . probably are . . . afraid. But you've made my life immensely better already."

I don't know if it was being an actor that made him so honest, so unafraid of being vulnerable, or if it was just who he was. I wished I could do the same, but that wasn't who *I* was.

"Can I ask you a question?"

His hand in my hair trailed across my jaw.

"Of course," he answered.

"Why did you take this job? Not that I'm not glad you are here, but you said yourself you were miserable."

"I was . . . not anymore." He leaned back in and kissed me again, humming as he pressed his lips against mine. It did not slip my notice that he hadn't answered my question, but I didn't care enough about the answer to stop kissing him, especially when his mouth finally opened, and I tasted sweet and mint and his breath mixed with mine.

His tongue slid against mine, and my hand beneath his shirt came back to life, curling around his side, pulling closer until my pelvis pressed into his hip. The kiss was leisurely and divine, but too slow, slow, slow.

I wanted more. I wanted our bodies flush, I wanted our lips crushed together, not softly teasing. I didn't want to lose the contact with his skin, but I wanted to take control. My other hand was trapped beneath me, propping me up on my side. So I slipped my hand out of his shirt and placed it on his face instead. I pulled him closer, trying to change the pace.

He allowed it for a moment, our lips moving faster, breath escaping as our heads tilted and our mouths battled. And God it was good. I kept pulling, not satisfied, not close enough, until he angled up and rolled onto his side to face me. A sigh of success escaped me, then he took the hand I had on his face and pulled it away, away, until it was trapped behind me, held there, pressed into my lower back by his hand.

Then again, he leaned back, changing the pace, brushing against my lips, slowly, softly. It was maddening. I tried leaning into him, but he held strong, pinning me back, taking his time. I groaned in frustration.

And he *smiled.*

"What is it, love?"

Any number of words could have come out of my mouth, some of them incoherent, most of them not very nice. Luckily, the ones I managed were exactly what I meant.

"Too slow," I whined.

I was actually *whining.*

"I told you I could do slow," he said.

"You jerk." That was actually one of the nicer words going through my head. He didn't even have the decency to be worried. He just laughed. I squirmed, trying to pull my arm free, and he appeased me with a kiss, this one a little harder, a little more satisfying than the last. And just when I was forgetting why I'd been so frustrated before, he pulled back again.

It was absurd, but I actually felt like I might cry. His lips trailed along my jaw to that spot below my ear that made every taut muscle in my body go limp.

"I wasn't trying to be smart," he whispered. "I'm trying to give you what you want. It's hard when I let myself go, when I kiss you how I want to. Because all I can think about then is how your skin tastes and how much I want to taste it again." His mouth burned against my neck. His teeth grazed against me, and on impulse, my hips surged forward, just barely making contact with him. He groaned in response, his whispers turning gruff, losing their softness. "I remember the weight of your breast in my hand, and the way you reacted to my fingers inside you." I bit my lip against the whimper building in my throat. I wanted his hands on me. I wanted our clothes off. "I think about having your body beneath me.

I think about being inside you. I think about it, and it con-
sumes me. And going slow is the very last thing to cross my
mind."

I lost it. I couldn't hold in the whimper, and I felt like I
was going to fall apart from his words alone.

"So I have to kiss you slowly. Unless you've changed your
mind. Have you? Changed your mind?"

Yes! Please, oh God, yes.

This was like torture.

But reason unfurled in the back of my mind, taking
over, keeping me grounded. What if we tried to have sex and
I chickened out again and I ruined everything?

"No, I haven't changed my mind," I said, then added,
"you jerk," because that *was* torture, and by the smile on his
face, he knew it.

"Hmmm . . . then slow it is."

19

was still a little angry with Garrick when I left that night, but when he walked me to my door and asked what I was doing the next day, I wasn't angry enough to blow him off. Cade wasn't speaking to me, and I hadn't heard from Kelsey, so I told him I was free, and we made plans for dinner at my place.

I slept in until noon, my bed too comfortable to be able to pry myself out of it. Then I distracted myself with an extra-long shower, followed by homework, then a book. When I checked the clock, it was still only 3:00 P.M.

I grabbed my computer and searched "Philadelphia theatre."

I found a theatre alliance website that gave info on a bunch of theatres in the city, as well as job postings and auditions. I clicked through, seeing what shows were currently running where, reading job descriptions, and bookmarking a few pages.

My cell rang, but it sounded far off. I tried following the sound, but the ringing ended before I was able to narrow my search down further than somewhere in the living room. Luckily, whoever was calling was persistent and called again a few moments later. It was definitely somewhere near the couch. I pulled back cushions, but found nothing. I checked under papers and books, still nothing. Finally, I dropped to the ground and peered under the couch. There it was, lighting up the dusty darkness beneath my furniture. And right beside it, glaring at me, was Hamlet.

That brief interlude of sweetness I'd seen from her at the shelter had yet to make another appearance. And I had no doubt that she'd somehow dragged my phone underneath there to spite me.

"Listen, cat, I don't know why you hate me so much, but you must have missed the memo. I *rescued* you." Flat on my stomach, I squeezed myself beneath the couch, reaching for my phone. "You're *supposed* to be thankful."

When my hand got closer, she let out her now-familiar low growl.

"Yeah, yeah, shut up."

I had to push half my body into the space between the couch and the floor to reach my phone, and getting out was even more uncomfortable than getting in.

2 missed calls from MOM.

I groaned. I should have just left it under the couch. At

that moment it rang again, for the third time. I answered, "Hi, Mom."

"Why didn't you answer the first two times? Is everything okay?"

"I'm fine, Mom. I just couldn't find my phone."

"Oh, well, you should really have a spot that you put it every time you come home. That way you always know where it is."

"I'll keep that in mind, Mom."

"So, your disorganization is old news. What else is happening in your life?" I swear, my mother was the only person in the world who didn't think I was a neurotic control freak because she was infinitely worse. She asked the inevitable question: "Have you met anyone?"

I rolled my eyes, which I never could have gotten away with face to face.

"I'm pretty busy with school, Mom. I actually just got cast as a lead in a play."

"Oh, that's nice," she said mildly. She thought going into theatre was a waste of my intelligence.

"It's actually kind of a big deal."

"Of course it is, honey. You just know how your father and I worry. We'd feel so much better if you had someone to take care of you financially."

There was a knock at the door, and I went to answer it as I spoke. "First of all, financial security is not a good enough reason to get married, Mother, even if it makes *you* feel better. Secondly, I don't need a guy to take care of me. I can take care of myself." Garrick was on the other side of the door, almost an hour early, and he got to hear the tail end of my speech. He raised an eyebrow, smiling, and if I could have reached through my phone to throttle my mother, I would have. "Anyway, I need to go, Mom. I have company."

"Is it male company?"

I groaned and said, "Good-bye."

Hanging up felt so good. I was tempted to call her back and do it a second time.

Garrick smiled. "Your mum sounds a lot like mine."

I glared at him. "You're early." I'd just pulled my hair into a wet ponytail that morning. I'd been planning on straightening it before he came, but now I just looked frumpy. And after crawling under the couch, I was dusty too.

"Is that okay?"

It would probably be pretty rude to tell him to go home and come back in an hour.

"No, it's fine. You can watch TV or something. I just need a second." I waved him into the living room and slipped into my bedroom, wondering how much improvement I could do in five minutes.

I pulled the band out of my hair and looked at the wavy, damp mess I had to work with. There was no time to dry it and straighten it. And if I dried it without straightening it, I'd have a fluff-ball for hair. I used my hands to mess it up a little more, scrunching it up in my hands, hoping the curly look would do. I worked a little bit of mousse into it, but that was all I had time for. I put on a quick coat of mascara and some Chapstick, hoping he was okay with the au naturel look.

When I came out of my room, Garrick was stretched out on my couch, watching TV, and Hamlet was curled into a tight ball on his chest. I stood there in shock, certain I was dreaming.

He turned and saw me watching. "Hey, your hair is curly." I nodded. I almost always wore it straight. He said, "I like it."

I was still stuck on the fact that my cat was perched happily on his chest . . . *purring.* He had magic powers. That was the only answer.

"Come here," he said, sitting up and shifting Hamlet into his lap. I sat down gingerly, a few feet away.

I pointed at Hamlet and said, "How did you do that?"

"Do what?"

"Get her to let you hold her."

"It's a her?" he asked.

"Yes, and she hates everyone. Especially me."

"Your own cat hates you?"

"We're working out our issues."

He laughed. "Maybe she's miffed that you gave her a boy's name."

I reached out a hand to pet her and, as always, received a growl for my troubles. Garrick thought Hamlet's hatred of me was hilarious. And he kept holding her, which meant I was relegated to the opposite cushion because my cat had stolen my . . . whatever he was.

Ugh. That was something I didn't want to think about. I mean, obviously, it was a secret relationship, so it wasn't like we necessarily needed labels, but I *was* curious. What would happen when the year was up? Would we even last that long?

I got up to start dinner to distract myself.

I made spaghetti because it was the only thing I trusted

myself not to screw up when I was nervous. And, well, I was always nervous around Garrick. He apparently had the opposite effect on Hamlet, who was fast asleep in his lap.

I saw my window of opportunity for what I'd been craving since he arrived.

I left the food cooking on the stove and made my way to the couch. I didn't sit for fear of waking up the moody one, but I placed a hand on Garrick's shoulder and leaned down for a kiss. Since his hands were trapped beneath Hamlet, I got to control the kiss. My hands found his hair, which was as addicting and soft as always, and the kiss deepened. I kissed him hard, because I could, and he made no effort to stop me. It was the kiss I'd wanted the night before that he'd refused to give me.

I didn't want to pull back, but I did have dinner on. His eyes were dark when we separated. "I think you might be a little evil," he said.

I laughed. "Yes, I planned all of this. Hamlet was in on it as well."

"Kiss me again."

He didn't have to ask me twice.

Every time we kissed, my confidence grew stronger. The longer I knew him, the bolder I became. I liked it . . . almost as much as I liked him.

Someone knocked on the door, three loud raps, followed by three more only seconds later. Our breath was still short from the kiss, and I wasn't sure if the too-quick thump of my heart was due to Garrick or the shock.

"Are you expecting someone?" he whispered.

I shook my head.

Three more knocks, and then Kelsey yelled through the door, "I know you're here, Bliss! Open up!"

"Shit."

I made no effort to be gentle as I picked Hamlet up from Garrick's lap and plopped her on the couch. I almost didn't even notice the growl; it had become so commonplace.

I grabbed Garrick and pulled him to his feet. I had no idea where to put him, but decided the bathroom was probably better than the bedroom, seeing as it actually had a door.

I pushed him inside with a quick "I'm sorry. I'll get rid of her, I promise."

If only we had gone to his place.

I rubbed at my lips, hoping they weren't as swollen as they felt. I ran a hand over my hair, and when I was certain there was nothing glaringly out of place, I opened the door.

Kelsey breezed past me, "It's about damn time. What were you doing?"

I faked a yawn.

"Oh, you know, just lazing around."

She rolled her eyes and looked at me like *I* was the frustrating one.

"It's a good thing I came over then. I'm not about to let you stay home on a Saturday night moping about the thing with Cade."

She snatched my wrist and pulled me into my bedroom. So the bathroom had been the right choice.

"I'm not moping!" I said. "And how do you know about the thing with Cade?"

"Because everyone knows, honey. Which, btw, I'm pissed that you didn't tell me all that drama was happening."

Great.

"There's really not that much drama. We'll patch things up soon, I'm sure," I said.

"Oh, honey, you didn't hear? Cade almost turned down the role in *Phaedra*. He didn't, thank God. Rusty talked him out of it. But I wouldn't call that 'not much drama.' "

I sank onto my bed, my insides twisting like a wrung-out rag. Cade was that upset? He would give up that great of a part just so that he didn't have to be around me?

Kelsey's voice came to me from my closet, and I had déjà vu of the night that this whole thing started. She started pulling out tops and skirts, and I asked, "What are you doing?"

"We're going out. You need to remember that a world exists outside your apartment."

"No, Kelsey, I'd really rather not." I thought about Garrick in my bathroom and wondered if he could hear us.

"Tough shit. I'm not giving you a choice. I haven't been dancing forever, and I need a wing-woman."

I groaned and flopped back on my bed. She dropped a skirt on my face.

"Get dressed."

Then I remembered the perfect excuse. "I can't. I've got dinner cooking."

"Great. I'm starving. What are we having?"

Sometimes I thought my life would be easier if I were friendless.

I returned to the kitchen, and she followed. I'd left the sauce on a little too long, and it had burned around the edges. So much for not screwing up spaghetti.

"Geez, woman, were you planning to eat away your

troubles? You made enough for three people!" I just shrugged. I had nothing to explain why I was cooking for two people (one with a very large appetite).

I put a little bit of spaghetti on our plates, trying to leave some for Garrick, even though I had no idea when he'd get to eat it.

I ate quickly, letting Kelsey dominate the conversation, which was about how long it had been since she'd had really good sex. I nodded along, laughing in the right places, shoveling food into my mouth the entire time. I cleared my plate before she'd even made a dent in hers. I placed my plate in the sink and then headed for the hallway.

"Where are you going?" Kelsey asked.

I called "Bathroom!" over my shoulder and kept walking.

When I reached the door, I glanced over my shoulder, glad to find Kelsey preoccupied with her spaghetti, and I slipped inside the room.

"Is she gone?" Garrick asked.

"Ssshhh!" He was leaning against the sink, and I reached around him to turn on the faucet to cover our whispers. "No. I'm sorry. She's actually eating our spaghetti."

His lips puckered, and I leaned forward, smothering my laugh against his chest.

"Is she leaving soon?"

I peered up at him, but stayed close against him.

"No. She thinks I'm depressed about Cade, and she's determined to force me to go out."

He pulled me to him and pressed his face into the space where my neck curved into my shoulder. He let out a growl that was oddly reminiscent of Hamlet.

I wrapped my arms around him, just as disappointed. "I know. This sucks."

As if I'd given him the idea, his lips covered my pulse point, sucking softly. I laughed and pushed him back.

"Garrick, she's right outside."

As if on cue, Kelsey knocked at the door.

"Enough stalling, chica! I've picked out your outfit!" The doorknob started turning, and I rushed to intercept her.

I kept my foot in the way so that only a crack of space formed.

I said, "I'm not stalling, just getting ready. Hand me the clothes, and I'll get changed."

She looked suspicious at my feigned excitement. I was never excited when she dragged me out like this. I kept smiling, like maybe the stress had gotten to me, and I'd just finally cracked.

She passed me the clothes, and before she had a chance to reply, I pushed the door closed and locked it as quietly as I could.

When I turned around, Garrick was slumped on the toilet. I switched on the radio, turning it up as loud as I could stand, and turned off the faucet.

"I'm sorry, Garrick."

Sitting, his head was level with my chest, and he rested his hands on my hips, pulling me forward.

"It's okay, darling. This was bound to happen sooner or later."

"I wish you could come with me."

"Me too. But it's okay. We'll have dinner another time.

You should get changed. The sooner you get out of here, the less likely we are to get caught."

I nodded. My hands shook slightly as I pulled the clothes to my chest.

He said, "I'll close my eyes." And I dropped a quick, thankful kiss on his cheek.

Smiling, he closed his eyes and then leaned his elbows on his knees and his face into his hands. As quickly as I could, I whipped off my shirt and shrugged off my shorts. I pulled a black tank top over my head and then picked up the skirt.

My stomach dropped.

It was that god-awful, horrendously short miniskirt. I must have made a noise, because Garrick raised his head. He kept his eyes closed as he asked, "Everything okay?"

I said, "Yes."

Even though I was thinking, *Hell no.*

I slipped on the skirt, and it was just as short as I remembered. I sighed. There was no way I could wear this.

I touched Garrick's shoulder, meaning to tell him that I was going to go outside to find something else, but his eyes opened and fixed on my legs, which suddenly felt weak, like pools of fabric instead of muscle and flesh and bone.

One of his hands curled around to tickle at the back of my knee, and I had to steady myself with a hand on his shoulder to keep from collapsing.

"You're trying to kill me, aren't you?" he choked. "Isn't this the skirt you told me you'd never wear?"

"And I won't be wearing it tonight. I'm going back to my room to find something else."

I turned, and his other hand touched my thigh. "Wait."

His hands trailed up to the indecently short hem and around to the back of my thighs, inches below the curve of my butt.

"You. Are. *Unbelievably.* Sexy." His voice was so low it rumbled, and I could feel the vibrations soaking into my skin. He leaned down and punctuated each word with a chaste kiss up the side of my thigh. I could have been clay in his hands, the way he was controlling me. If he had tried, I might have given up my virginity to him there in the bathroom without much of a fight.

But Kelsey's fist pounded on the door, snapping me out of my lust.

"Damn, Bliss. Would you hurry it up already?"

With her words, my fear came back. Sure, he thought I was sexy now. But virgins were pretty much the least sexy things ever. Would he change his mind when he found out?

"I have to go. I'm sorry. There's probably spaghetti still left over if you want some after we leave. I'll . . . I'll call you, okay?"

He nodded, his eyes still dark, unwavering.

I tumbled out into the hallway, a mess of hormones and emotions. I was so distracted that I didn't even remember that I'd intended to change until I was already buckled into Kelsey's car and we were on our way to the club.

20

Ecstasy, the club, was dark and hazy when we entered. The beat of the music pounded through the walls and the floor, seeping into my skin, setting me on edge. This wasn't my scene at all, but Kelsey loved it. I figured all I had to do was hang out at the bar, maybe chat with a guy or two, so she'd get off my back. Then she'd probably go home with some guy and leave me her car. That's how these things usually went.

What I hadn't anticipated was the way my change in attire would change the normal plan. We were barely in the door for a minute before a guy had asked me to dance. I declined, which earned me a glare from Kelsey.

"What?" I shouted over the music. "You said I had to come, not that I had to dance!"

We stood at the bar, and I worked to flag down a bartender while Kelsey berated me.

"You are the most infuriating person I have ever met! You look smoking hot tonight, and all you're going to do is sit over here and pout like always!"

"Then maybe you should have let me stay *home* and pout!"

A guy tapped on my shoulder, and I didn't even wait for him to ask before I said, "*No!*"

Kelsey fixed her hands on her hips. For a Barbie look-alike, she was still pretty intimidating. "I realize you are upset, and you've got a lot going on. I'm trying to be understanding, but what is your *problem?*"

"I don't have a problem, Kelsey. I just don't like that you think you can drag me places without any concern for what I actually want!"

"Fine! Never mind! I give up! Sit here and pout! I'm going to dance!"

She spun around and pushed through the crowd, spilling several drinks and knocking people out of her way.

Scary Barbie.

I inched onto a stool, conscious of the fact that my short skirt made it so that my bare legs were glued to the plastic. I wouldn't have been surprised if my ass was hanging out, but at the moment I was too pissed off to care. I ordered a Jack and Coke and sat there seething while I waited for it to come. I knew Kelsey meant well, but the solution to all the world's problems was not partying. I'd always known we were very different people, but I'd never realized just how much she didn't understand me.

"Can I buy you a drink?" a voice asked over my shoulder. I held up my full drink and ignored him.

The guy took a seat beside me anyway. He leaned in to ask me something else, and I snapped, "I'm not interested!"

Then a familiar voice answered, "I'm glad to hear that."

I nearly fell off my stool when I picked up the accent.

"Garrick!"

Garrick was sitting next to me, a cap pulled down low over his eyes, covering his gorgeous blond hair.

He hadn't sounded like Garrick when he'd first spoken. "You sounded—"

When he answered this time his accent was gone and he sounded American. No particular dialect, just . . . normal. "I am an actor, Bliss. I know how to cover my accent."

Still in shock, I asked, "What are you doing here? What if someone sees you?"

"I'm incognito, sort of. And if anyone does, I'll just say we ran into each other by chance. I'm a professor. I didn't take a vow to have zero social life."

"But why?"

"Because I couldn't stomach the thought of you dancing with anyone else in that skirt." His hand grazed my thigh, and all the heat from earlier came rushing back.

"Garrick, stop! Someone is going to see! What if Kelsey comes back?"

"Based on the show you guys put on earlier, I don't see that happening anytime soon."

I cringed. Maybe I had been a little bitchy.

"Come on." He stood up and offered me a hand. I looked

around, scared to take it. It was so dark. If there was someone here we knew, we would have no way of knowing unless we came face to face. This was too big of a chance.

"Stop thinking so much," he told me and wrapped an arm around my waist to slide me off the seat. The bare skin of my thighs squeaked embarrassingly against the seat, but he didn't seem to notice or care. He threaded our fingers together and pulled me into the crowd.

I kept my head down, concentrating on putting my feet where his had just been. He led me down a few steps onto a lower level where it was somehow even darker and the bodies were pressed tighter together. I couldn't see anyone but the people right next to me. He weaved and pulled until we were in the farthest corner, then pulled me between him and the wall. His back was to the rest of the room, and his tall form covered me completely.

His breath tickled against my ear as he whispered, "Better?"

I nodded. It was better. I mean, we were still in a club and I would rather have been at home alone, but already this was the best club experience I'd ever had.

Even knowing how he felt about me, I was too nervous to dance with him face to face. So I turned until my back was pressed against his front. His hands went immediately to my hips, pulling me against him. The sensation chased all the air out of my lungs.

I closed my eyes so I didn't have to stare at the wall, and I tried to let the music swoop through me. Slowly, his hips tilted forward, and I followed, pushing back against him. He exhaled against my ear, and it sent shivers down my spine. He slid a hand from my hip to my stomach. With his fingers splayed, his thumb rested about an inch below my bra and his pinky trailed the waistband of my skirt. He used that hand to pull me in to him at the same time that he rolled his hips.

Stars danced behind my closed eyes, and my heartbeat matched the steady thrum of the music. His body against mine seemed to heat up the already sweltering room, and I felt sweat begin to dampen my neck. His hips kept rolling to the music, slowly and sensually, but every once in a while, on a strong beat, his hips would push harder against mine. His lips touched the skin of my neck, and I was falling, falling, falling into the feeling.

It wasn't enough. Would I ever have enough of him? I reached my hands up and behind me, tangled them in his hair, and he hummed his approval. The hand on my stomach came up, running lightly from my raised arm down my side. He grazed the side of my breast, and the touch sent tremors through me, which were amplified when his fingers passed the indecent skirt and gripped my thigh.

The song changed, but we didn't. His hands kept driving me crazy. Our bodies stayed tightly pressed together. I was still so turned on, I felt dizzy with want. The whole world was spinning, and only we were still. Or maybe it was us who were spinning. All I knew was that there was everyone else and then there was us, and I never wanted it to be any other way.

He found that spot below my ear, and I moaned, glad for the music that swallowed the sound. He nipped at my neck with his teeth, and I dug my fingernails into his neck in response.

"God, Bliss, do you have any idea how badly I want you?"

Our hips rolled again, and I was certain I had a pretty good idea.

The song ended, and I'd had about all I could take. I slipped my phone out of my bra, where it had been conveniently tucked. Garrick groaned and pulled our hips together again in response, but I was focused on my phone. My hands were shaking, but I still managed to type out a text to Kelsey.

Met someone. Leaving. Sry abt earlier. Talk 2 u tom?

I didn't wait for a reply before I pulled Garrick toward the exit.

For once, I didn't care how fast we went on his motorcycle. I just held on tight and tried to will us home faster.

His lips were on my neck before I even got the key in my door. My breathing was so heavy, it could only have been called panting. When I finally got the door open, I pushed it so hard that it slammed against the wall. I'd have to check the next day and make sure there wasn't a hole. As soon as the door was closed, we were kissing.

I had tugged my heels off between the motorcycle and my door, and now, without them, he was too far away. The thought must have occurred to us at the same time, because his hands left my thighs and cupped my ass, lifting me so that I had to wrap my legs around his waist.

My back slammed against the door, and I gasped. His tongue snaked into my mouth, plunging in and out, fast and hard—exactly the way I liked it.

"Bed," I gasped between kisses.

He leaned back long enough to say, "Are you sure?" Then we were kissing again, and the rhythm he set was just as seductive and hypnotizing as the music had been in the club. He asked again, "Bliss, are you sure?"

Was I sure? Why was he asking me questions? Did he realize I just wanted to kiss him? I wanted to kiss him until the rest of the world fell away.

"Bed," I said again.

"That's not an answer." He moved toward the bedroom anyway.

I clung to him tightly, transferring my kisses to his jaw and then his neck so that he could concentrate on walking.

Somehow I still managed to get caught in the curtains.

Like, literally caught.

My earring caught on the sheer material, and I didn't notice until he kept walking. Pain lanced through my ear and the side of my head. I yelped in response.

"What? I'm sorry! What's wrong? What did I do?"

"Ear." Apparently I'd been reduced to one-word sentences.

"Damn. Hold still."

He tried to use both hands to free my earring, but then we lost our balance, and both of us slammed into the side of my dresser, which sat just inside my bedroom.

Judging by the way my elbow was smarting, I was going to have one hell of a bruise in the morning.

When the pain subsided, I laughed because, as usual, my life was ridiculous. And as luck would have it, it was one of those half-laugh half-snort hybrids. We both laughed, gasping for breath for an entirely different reason now. My side was aching from where we hit the dresser. My earring was still attached to the curtain, and my legs were still around his waist. Between laughs, Garrick pressed a sweet kiss to my forehead.

Maybe ridiculous wasn't so bad.

"Okay, let's get you untangled. I'm going to put you down, okay?"

He lowered me gently to the floor, and my stampeding pulse began to slow. He tried for a few minutes to free me, but his fingers were large and clumsy. Finally, I said, "Just undo the earring. I'll get it out of the curtain tomorrow."

Laughing, he did as I asked.

Before, I'd felt like I was burning up in our kiss. Now, warmth spread through me that was different, sweeter. Candlelight instead of open flame.

He rubbed at the shoulder that had hit the dresser and said, "We're kind of a mess."

I pinched my fingers together and said, "Little bit."

He curled a hand around my neck and pulled me forward, pressing another kiss to my forehead. I closed my eyes, thinking that this was what perfection felt like.

"I think maybe the curtain did us a favor. Your legs in that skirt pretty much killed all my self-control."

I smiled. "I told you that I never should have worn it."

"Oh, I'm definitely glad you wore it. It's a memory I'll cherish for a very long time." I slapped him on the arm, but I didn't mind the cheeky smile. He said, "I should probably go now, before you make me lose my mind again."

I let him go, even though a large part of me was screaming in protest. And when he was gone, I celebrated in much the same way I had done when I learned I'd gotten cast as Phaedra.

I danced.

Because . . . finally . . . things were going right.

21

Things were *so* wrong.

The first *Phaedra* read-through was a disaster of epic proportions. Even after two weeks, Cade wouldn't speak to me at all before we started, and it seemed like everyone in the cast was on his side, based on the glares I was getting. And even though read-throughs tend to be a bit stale, since everyone is sitting around a table, this one was worse than week-old pizza.

Every once in a while, Eric would shake his head, and I could practically see him thinking, *What happened to the people I cast last week?*

Each scene kept getting worse, like a screw going in at the

wrong angle, but we just kept going, trying to make something work that would clearly not.

When it was over, I felt deflated. I had been so excited about this play. I'd been waiting for something like this since freshman year, and now it was here and it was unbearable.

Eric faked some optimism, saying things would be smoother onstage. I don't think anyone believed him.

And if they did, that misplaced hope dwindled when we had our first rehearsal onstage, which, if possible, was even worse. The unease between Cade and me seemed to permeate the entire cast until everyone was stiff and on edge.

Classes weren't much better.

Cade stayed far away from me, and Kelsey was still angry, so I was disproving that quote about no man being an island. I was totally alone.

Except for Garrick.

I was terrified by the depth of my feelings for him. Things were too good. Nothing in life was this amazing, at least not in my life. He stopped me after Senior Prep Wednesday morning. "Bliss, wait one second."

I took my time packing up my stuff, waiting for everyone else to leave the computer lab. When we were alone, I asked, "What's up?"

He smiled, "Nothing."

Then he pressed me into the computer table behind me and kissed me.

I gasped in shock, and his tongue stormed my mouth. I did nothing but blink, and then he had me lifted up onto the table, his hips fitted between my open thighs, his mouth burning against my own.

There was no slowness to this kiss. It was a frenzied, stolen moment, and I was spinning with want. I clung to him, certain I was about to fall to pieces in his arms, and then he pulled back.

I had to concentrate on breathing for several long seconds before it even occurred to me to be mad. I swatted his bicep. "Are you crazy? What were you thinking? What if someone walked in?" I pushed him several feet away and hopped off the table, my legs unsteady against the floor.

"I was thinking that you looked entirely too sexy for this early in the morning."

I steeled my glare. "I'm serious, Garrick."

"So am I," he said. He took me by the elbow and pulled me into the far corner of the room, where we couldn't be seen from the door and we'd have warning if anyone entered. "When it comes to you, Bliss, I'm very serious."

Was he implying what I thought he was implying? The look in his eyes was dangerous. I couldn't think straight when he was so close to me. He tried to pull me into another kiss, but even out of sight from the door, I was too scared, too afraid. It felt like that first night together on my bed all over again. Was this me? Was I ready for something like this?

I turned my head, and his lips found my neck instead.

Everything was just so confusing.

How could I want something so badly and not want it at the same time?

A part of me wanted to fold my arms around him and pray for his lips never to leave my skin. And a part of me wanted to run screaming in the other direction.

The second part came out on top.

I pulled out of his embrace and held up a hand to keep him from following me. "I can't. I have to go. I want to try and find Cade before rehearsal tonight, see if we can't work things out."

Then I fled the lab, my skin still burning from his touch.

Cade was already gone by the time I made it to the greenroom, and I didn't manage to get him alone for the rest of the day. I thought about asking to talk to him before rehearsal, but everyone was around, staring, and I truthfully just didn't have the energy.

But that meant that our third rehearsal started just as poorly as all the rest.

Eric, who had no idea of the offstage drama, was at a loss. I think he could tell that it all stemmed from Cade and me, which was why he sent us away. He said he just wanted to spend some time with the chorus, but he still wanted us to get some work done. So he sent us into a smaller workshop space to work alone . . . with Garrick.

It had to be a sign of the apocalypse. Things this terrible only happened when the world was about to end.

I envied Garrick's composure. He didn't give anything away.

I, on the other hand, was a train wreck in human form.

We ran our first scene together twice. Cade was lifeless, and I was pitiful.

No matter how many times Garrick muttered between lines, "Wake up," or, "Intensity!" or "Raise the stakes!" we were still awful.

Garrick, who knew what we were both capable of, grew more and more frustrated. He didn't even bother faking optimism.

"Both of you take five."

I went to the bathroom and splashed my face with water. This had to stop. If I could act opposite Dom, I could certainly act opposite Cade, no matter how upset he was. He was my best friend, but I had to learn to put my emotions aside and think of him like anyone else if I wanted to be an actor.

Feeling a little better, I made my way back to the workshop room.

Cade and Garrick were already inside talking.

"I know there is personal stuff going on between the two of you, but you've got to get over it," Garrick said.

"I'm trying. It's not that simple."

Garrick's back was to me, but I could see Cade's face, which was pale and crumpled, like a discarded piece of paper. I choked up, wishing this was all over or that it had never happened.

"You're not trying hard enough. So she didn't return your feelings. That's life." My jaw dropped. How could he be so callous? Garrick, who had been so sweet and understanding when I'd come to him about this same fight? "It happens. You've got to grow up. Are you an actor or not? You can't let your feelings for her dictate your life."

My mouth went dry, and a hard lump formed in my throat.

I pushed the door open the rest of the way and said, "That's enough." The heat in my voice surprised me, but it shouldn't have. I hated seeing Cade hurt, and *finally* it wasn't just me causing it. Garrick's words had sunk under my skin, festering, and my hands were shaking with anger.

Cade looked horrified at seeing me.

Garrick didn't look guilty at all, which only made my anger burn hotter. I walked until I stood between the two guys, blocking Cade from sight.

"This is none of your business," I told Garrick.

He turned toward me, and his whole face seemed to pull down with his frown. "It is my business when you both bring your outside issues into rehearsal."

I knew, logically, that he was right. And I knew that he was my teacher and this was his job, but the judgment in his tone cut me all the same.

And I wanted to cut him back.

"You're probably right," I said. "Maybe relationships have no place here at all. It's a bad idea to mix them, don't you think?"

He was so calm, which made me want to shake him. I wanted to sink my fingers into his shoulder and shove and pull and push.

"Bliss, you're being unprofessional."

"*I'm being unprofessional?* Oh, that's rich, coming from you!"

"You and I can talk about this later." His hand touched my elbow, and I hated that, even when I was angry, his touch made my knees weak. I pulled away.

"I don't *want* to talk about this later. I just want you to direct. I want you to stay out of my business with Cade. Do you hear me? Do you understand? Stay out of it. That's *all* I want from you."

Finally, something in his calm expression cracked. His jaw clenched, and for a second he screwed his eyes shut. It didn't feel as good as I thought it would to see him affected. And already I wanted to take it back.

"Fine." He threw his hands up and repeated, "Fine. As a director, I'm telling both of you that you need to get your shit together before next rehearsal, unless you'd like us to start looking at your understudies. You're dismissed."

The door slammed on his way out, and I heard the echo again and again in my mind. I was so stupid. This was *so* stupid.

I'd almost completely forgotten Cade was there until he said, "Holy shit, Bliss. He's the guy?"

I could have denied it. I could have told him the whole story. I could have run. But I felt too hollowed out to move. I slumped onto my knees, wrapping my arms around my middle like that would somehow hold me together, like if I held hard enough, the pain wouldn't creep in.

But it did.

And the empty spaces in me were suddenly full of the words I regretted and the shame I felt and the absence of him. There was nothing more to do but cry.

It streamed from me slow and steady, rising like the tide, washing away everything I'd loved about our time together.

A hand touched my shoulder, and I spun around, hoping.

It was Cade.

Slow and unsure, he knelt beside me and took me in his arms. I hesitated for a moment, knowing how he felt, knowing how hard this must be for him, knowing that as usual he was too good to me.

Then I couldn't resist anymore. I was already selfish, what was the harm?

I burrowed into his arms and let go. It was the ugly cry of all ugly cries, but I didn't care. Because my capacity to ruin good things knew no bounds.

"It's okay," Cade told me. "It wasn't that bad."

"Wasn't that bad?" I rubbed at my eyes, and my hands came back smeared black. "Maybe in comparison to the Holocaust. But as breakups go, I think it was pretty bad."

He stiffened. "You guys were together? Like *really* together?"

"For a couple weeks, technically, before I ruined it." God, no wonder I was a virgin. I must have broken a whole world of mirrors in a past life.

Against all odds, he had actually liked me. Despite the fact that I ran out on him during sex with a terrible excuse. Despite the fact that I still wouldn't sleep with him. Despite how horrendously fucking awkward I was. He liked *me*. I sobbed again, because it wasn't fair.

"You like him a lot, don't you?"

Struggling for breath, I nodded. "I do. I know it's crazy. I know it's stupid. But, but . . . we met before he was our professor, and I can't just turn it off. I tried. We tried. I guess I'll *have* to turn it off now."

Cade rocked me back and forth, and even though it was nice, it made me feel young and immature. Unprofessional, just like Garrick had said.

"He'll forgive you," Cade said. "I would."

I wanted to ask if that meant Cade forgave me now, but I was too afraid. So I stayed in his arms, crying and quiet, just in case this was only a temporary reprieve, in case this was all I would get.

By the time we left the studio, rehearsal was over and everyone else had left. He walked me out to my car, and I started to hope . . . to hope that maybe we'd be okay. He didn't kiss me on the cheek like he would have before. He rested a hand on my shoulder. And though it was different, it was enough.

"It will be okay," he said. And I hoped he was talking about everything . . . about us, about Garrick, about life.

I needed everything to be okay.

22

thought about going to his place as soon as I got home, but truth be told, I was afraid. And it was so much easier just to feel sorry for myself. I had a tub of chocolate chip cookie dough ice cream in my freezer on hold for just such occasions. It would have been nice to share it with Kelsey, but I couldn't afford to share my secret with another person, and I wasn't selfish enough to make Cade witness any more of my pity party. He promised he wouldn't tell anyone, and I believed him.

I sat on one end of my couch, eyeing Hamlet spread out on the other end. I wondered if she might comfort me. She had been nice to me only once at another sad moment, so maybe I had a chance. I reached for her and received not just her usual growl but a hiss too.

She was clearly on Garrick's side.

I thought about going to him a thousand times, maybe a thousand and one. But I had to face it—he had been out of my league from the very beginning. He would have gotten tired of me eventually, once the forbidden factor wore off. And I couldn't even begin to contemplate what might have happened if we'd been caught. Even the thought of it brought adrenaline rushing through me, like when he'd kissed me in the lab for anyone to see. Maybe I was doing myself a favor, severing the ties now. I mean, it sucked times seven billion, but it would have been worse after more time.

In my dim, quiet apartment in my ice cream—induced haze, I could admit that I had been falling for him. Our oh-so-brief relationship had been like spending a day in sunlight when you've lived your whole life underground (my former self being the mole man in this story). Maybe that was all we got when it came to relationships like that—flashes of sunlight. Maybe it was too bright to be sustained for any extended period of time. Maybe I should have been thankful.

I didn't feel thankful. I felt miserable (and full of ice cream).

We were in the lab again Wednesday, and he never came within three feet of my workspace. At rehearsal that night he sat in the top row taking notes and never said a word.

Thursday and Friday were the same. The acting in rehearsals had improved now that Cade and I had sort of patched things up. We weren't quite friends again. I didn't see us hanging out alone anytime in the future, but we could talk without any major disasters, and both of our minds had cleared enough to focus on the play.

I returned to my mole man state on the weekend, never leaving my apartment, showering only when absolutely necessary. Any other weekend Kelsey might have forced me into an outing, but she was still a little ticked about my attitude at the club.

So I was pretty much alone.

I had no one but Hamlet. Who hated me with the fire of a thousand suns.

I passed an entire week in a state of loneliness before I had the nerve to do anything about it.

I dropped by during Garrick's office hours, too afraid to confront him at home or after class. When I approached the door, he was on the phone.

"I know." He was nodding, smiling. "I know. I'll be home before you know it. What is it, just three more months?"

I froze. I plastered myself to the wall outside his door, and my lungs seemed empty no matter how many breaths I took.

"That? No, I'm over it. It really wasn't anything to begin with . . . just inconvenient."

Something was crumbling inside me, something that had already been vulnerable and weak but now was breaking and breaking.

"I should have known better. I know, but it's over now, and I don't really care anymore, you know? Yeah, yeah. I'll find another place to work. It's just not worth it."

Not worth it?

I think, until then, I'd still hoped, even though I'd tried to talk myself out of it.

Hope . . . it was such a motherfucker.

I wouldn't cry. He was over it. I needed to be over it too. And I needed to make sure he knew it. If he was thinking about quitting to stay away from me, I had to fix that. I wouldn't be the reason he left.

Before I could change my mind, I reached out and knocked on the door frame and stepped into the open doorway.

He looked up and stuttered over whatever he was going to say next. He stared at me for a second, the phone forgotten in his hand.

Then, finally, he blinked and turned back to his conversation.

"Hey, I have to go. I'll call you later, okay?"

I hated whoever was on the other end of that phone call. Was it a girl? Did he have a girlfriend back in Philly? Had it been just a fling for him, just sex (or, well, almost sex)? Whoever it was spoke for another twenty seconds while he said "yes" and "okay" and nodded along.

When he hung up, I still had no idea what I was going to say.

He just looked at me for a moment, and then he said, "How can I help you, Bliss?"

His formal tone made me queasy, but I tried to copy it as best I could. "I just wanted to apologize for my behavior during our rehearsal together. Cade and I have worked everything out—"

He interrupted, "I noticed."

My thoughts stuttered, fleeing for the moment. "So . . . I, uh, I promise it won't happen again. In the future, I will maintain a professional attitude. I won't bring my personal life into rehearsal or your classroom."

He put down the pen he'd been toying with and started to stand. "Bliss . . ."

Whatever he was going to say, I couldn't hear it. If I had to listen to him try to let me down easy (when I knew he didn't care), I would end up crying and making a fool of myself. So I cut him off.

"It's okay. I'm over it. No big deal, right?"

He paused, and I was certain he knew I was lying, certain he could see into my churning stomach, my wringing heart. I willed him to believe me.

I'm okay. I'm over it. I'm okay. Okay. Okay.

"Right," he finally said.

I sucked in a greedy breath.

"Great. Thanks for your time. Have a nice day!" Then I was out the door and running, running, running down the stairs, out into the air where I could gulp and fill my lungs until I no longer felt like crying.

From then on I built walls with smiles and closed myself off with laughs. I made up with Kelsey, promising her I would go dancing whenever she wanted. I threw myself into rehearsal, memorizing all of my lines over a week before the off-book date. I willed myself into March like a soldier, moving forward, refusing to look back. Eric praised my work in rehearsals, saying he could feel my shame, my self-hatred in every word, could see it even in my posture. I smiled and pretended like I was glad to hear it.

I set my sights on graduation, when I would leave and go who knows where. Maybe I'd max out a credit card and go traveling with Kelsey. Maybe I'd go back home and work, save some money. Mom would just *love* that. Maybe I'd stay here, get a job at Target or something. I just had to get to the end. Things would get easier then. Then . . . I would deal. I'd tell Kelsey about everything, and we'd party the pain away. Then.

I couldn't wait for Then.

It seemed possible. It seemed doable.

Until the Now screwed everything up.

We were one week away from spring break—a much-needed break. Friday afternoon had us all in the black box theatre for Beginning Directing scene workshops. The entire department was gathered in the theatre—the junior directors were petrified while everyone else ranged from bored to sadistically gleeful.

I was just marching forward, willing the time to pass, until Rusty stood to make an announcement before the first scene.

Clearing his throat, he was remarkably serious for Rusty. "So . . . I went to the doctor yesterday."

"And you're pregnant?" someone at the back shouted.

"No," he said with a smile, albeit a small one. "Actually . . . I have mono."

There was a beat before it sank in.

"The doctor said that the incubation is anywhere be-tween four and eight weeks, which means I could have had it as far back as January or February. So . . . you might want to be careful about drinking after people and . . . other things."

January or February. The party. I'd kissed Rusty at that party. We'd all kissed . . . everyone.

By instinct, my eyes sought out the other players of that spin-the-bottle game. Their expressions were just as anxious and fearful as my own. If Rusty was already contagious back then, that meant I would have it, along with Cade, and Kelsey and Victoria, and every other person at that party.

And Garrick.

Damn.

23

I caught up to him as soon as the scenes were over. Actors milled about, still in their costumes. Professors congratulated their students, and everyone gravitated toward their group, making plans for the weekend. Everyone else seemed calm and happy, and I felt like the world was ending. Walking toward Garrick was up there with walking into a room filled with anthrax.

But I did it anyway.

Luckily, he wasn't talking to anyone, just checking something on his phone. I stood behind him for a few moments. Just being this close to him affected me. It really was like a poison. I breathed him in, and I could feel it breaking down the walls and protection I'd built.

I don't know if I made a noise or if he felt me behind him, but he turned and looked at me. For a split second, I thought he would smile. Then his expression changed, and he became wary. Like he didn't trust me. Then his face went blank.

I had all these emotions and memories pushing against my barricades, trying to spill out into the open. He looked like he couldn't care less.

I wanted to spit it out and run, but I knew that was a bad idea. It's not exactly normal to warn your professor that you might have given him mono.

"Can we talk . . . in private?" I asked.

He looked around the room, and I could imagine where his eyes went. To Eric probably. Maybe to Cade. Or Dom. Whatever he was looking at, he stayed focused there as he said, "I don't think that's a good idea, Bliss."

Yeah, I'd run out of good ideas a long time ago.

"It won't take long," I promised him.

He looked at me finally. I wanted to believe I saw a softness in his eyes, but I could have imagined it. I did that all the time. All I had to do was close my eyes and I could see him reaching toward me, his lips millimeters from my own. But always . . . always I opened my eyes and it wasn't real.

A hand curved around my shoulder and pulled me into a hug. It was Eric. He started talking about rehearsals and costumes and spring break and all of these things I just didn't have room for in my head.

I looked at Garrick, smiling at his boss. His smile was tight, close-lipped. When was the last time I had seen that gorgeous grin?

Maybe I didn't have to tell him. I mean, I wasn't even sick.

It wasn't like he'd made out with anyone else from that party (I hoped). And if I never got sick, he never had to know. Plus, he clearly wanted to just forget our little fling ever happened. I mean, he'd talked about changing jobs, for Christ's sake. And ever since then, I'd been careful not to look at him too long or stand too close or give any indication that I wasn't as over this as he was. Because, as bad as things were, it would be infinitely worse if he were just gone altogether.

Yeah. I'd tell him if I had to. No need to bring it up if it wasn't actually an issue.

I excused myself, said good-bye to Eric and Garrick both. Then I went back to pretending. At least my education was getting put to some use, even if I never managed to do anything else with it. It had taught me how to lie.

The last day of school before spring break I woke up exhausted and so cold that I wore a sweater to Garrick's class, even though it was spring in Texas. It was pretty obvious what was going on, or it should have been, but I was so preoccupied with surviving the day and getting to the break that I pushed aside my unease.

Garrick let us go early, but not before saying, "Sorry to give you guys homework over the break, but when you come back, I want a definitive plan for what you're doing on May 23, which for those of you not looking at your calendar is the day after your graduation."

Dom snickered behind me, "Does still being drunk from the night before count as a definitive plan?"

I didn't even have the energy to roll my eyes.

"Some of you I will see tonight at rehearsal, and the rest—

have a great spring break! Don't get arrested or married or any of that kind of thing! Enjoy the rest of your day."

I think there was clapping, but my head felt a little fuzzy. I packed up my things and decided I didn't really need to go to the rest of my classes. I needed to go home and take a nap. A nap sounded good. I'd be fine after I slept a little longer.

I felt dizzy as I tottered toward the door.

I hadn't realized everyone was gone until Garrick and I were alone and he asked, "Are you okay, Bliss?"

I nodded. My head felt like it was full of cotton.

"Just tired," I told him. I was coherent enough to make sure my response was carefully neutral—not needy or bitchy. "Thanks, though, have a good break!" My voice sounded far away, and it took all of my concentration to get out of the doors and to my car.

The drive home was a mystery. There had definitely been driving, but I couldn't remember the streets or ever turning the wheel until I was suddenly in front of my apartment, so close to my bed.

I wanted to fall right into it, but my neurotic need to hang a calendar right beside my bed reminded me that I had rehearsal later that night. I set one alarm for 5:00 P.M. so I'd have time to fix dinner beforehand, and I set another for 5:05 P.M. just in case I accidentally turned off the first. Then the bed caved in around me, and I was tumbling headlong into oblivion.

Minutes later the world was screaming, and it was so loud that I tried to press my hands against my ears, but they were dead, lifeless at my side. I swallowed, and my tongue felt barbed, my throat burned like chapped lips.

Rolling over felt like moving mountains.

The clock read 5:45 P.M.

I blinked and read it again.

5:45 P.M.

The world was still screaming and finally, *finally,* I lifted my hands and pushed at my alarm until the noise stopped.

I swallowed again, but my tongue felt too big. My spit singed like acid on its way down.

Dazed, I looked at the clock again. I was out of time. Rehearsal started in fifteen minutes. Somehow . . . I don't know how, really . . . I pushed myself out of bed. My legs quivered like the floor was a boat and beneath it the sea. There were things I needed to do . . . I knew that, but I couldn't think beyond that nagging sense that there was something I was missing. And it was so cold, where was my coat? I needed my coat.

Wrapped in the warmest things I could find, I lurched outside toward my car. The world turned for a second, like a child refusing to sit still. I stuck a hand out to steady myself, but there was nothing there to catch me. I pitched sideways. I didn't fall, but managed to catch myself, barely. I stared at the ground. I was just so tired. Would it be so bad to be there? On the ground?

It was so cold, though. I really should go inside if I was going to lie down . . . or in my car. Did I have time for a nap in my car?

I shook my head, trying to clear the fog, and something awful rattled around in my skull. It hurt. God, it hurt. I pressed at it with my hands, trying to understand why, and I swallowed again, which hurt too. Everything hurt. Everything.

I couldn't stand up anymore. Standing was too hard. I was almost to the ground, reaching for it, thinking the asphalt would be warm against my cheek, when something hooked me from behind.

I kept reaching, but I was caught, a fish dangling on a line.

I began to cry because my head was pounding and my throat was clamped down like iron. I still wanted my coat, and I didn't want to be a fish, and I wanted to sleep.

Sleep.

Someone was telling me that I was okay. The hook was gone, and my pillow held me once more, and I must have been dreaming. Sleep.

Sleep perchance to dream.

Something buzzed. I thought of bees. I was flying with bees.

". . . be okay. I can't tell how bad, but she definitely has a fever. She's not coherent at all. Mono, yeah. Should I take her to the hospital? Are you sure? You're sure. Okay. Yes. Bye. "

I reached a hand out. There were too many words. Bees shouldn't talk. That didn't make sense. Where was I?

"Where?" I groaned. Then, "Ow," because everything still hurt even after sleep. My hand found something. Or something found my hand. And it was warm. And I was freezing. I sighed. The warmth found my cheek, and I pushed into it, wanting more.

"So cold," I told the warmth.

And then the warmth answered, low and soft, "I don't know what to do."

I clutched the warmth that held my face and asked, "More."

Then the warmth left, even though I tried to hold on. Air blew past me, and I was shaking, shaking, shaking. I cried, and the tears felt like rivers of ice.

"Cold," I said. I swallowed, but that felt worse instead of better. I hated this. I wanted it to be over. Please. Please. Please.

"Please."

"I'm here, love. Hold on."

The world fell over, bent sideways, broken. And it cradled me, taking me with it, but instead of dying, I fell into warmth, solid and strong. I clutched at it, wanting to be inside it, to make the shaking stop, to make everything stop.

It was the sun, and it held me in its arms, called me by name, touched me from forehead to toes. I fell asleep cradled in the sky in the arms of a star.

When I woke next, my head was clear enough to know that I was sick. I had to breathe through my nose because my throat was too swollen, too tender to stand the passage of air. My muscles ached and my stomach felt hollow. I was still cold, but not frozen solid. Thawed. Sleep called me again. I was still so tired.

But I knew what that meant.

I had gotten mono after all.

Which meant I had to tell Garrick. But that could wait until my head wasn't bursting and my lungs felt full and my throat was not on fire. Once the fever broke, I would call him.

I shifted, wishing that my knees and my elbows and shoulders would just cease to exist because right now they were nothing but pain. And then I knew that I was dreaming, that the fever had rearranged my brain, because Garrick was there beneath me, his bare chest my pillow. It was cruel, this fever. But I knew it was only because I had thought of him. I was probably still dreaming.

His eyes were open, staring at me, not speaking, just staring. Couldn't be real.

"Wish it was real," I whimpered, before giving in again.

Sleeping.

Sleeping.

When I woke again, the chills had stopped, and I was alone. Even though I knew it was a dream, I pressed my face into my pillow, wishing it hadn't been.

I hadn't noticed until now, or maybe just hadn't admitted it, but even now I was falling for Garrick. Maybe I had never stopped falling. Every memory and fantasy pulled me deeper into wanting him. Though still exhausted, this time I had to work to fall back into sleep.

"Bliss, wake up."

No time had passed at all. It must have been a dream.

"You need to drink something. Wake up."

I tried to turn away, to crawl deeper into sleep, but something tugged against me, and I was sitting up against my will. Something pushed at my back, refusing to let me lie down, so instead I leaned sideways.

My head met something solid. It wasn't lying down, but it was close enough. I closed my eyes.

"Oh no, you don't. Drink first. Then you can sleep."

I was sleeping. At least, I thought I was. I must have been because out of nowhere a cup appeared in my hands. It was warm, almost as warm as the other hands wrapped around mine.

It smelled wonderful, and I let the cup be pulled to my lips.

Soup.

Chicken noodle maybe. It tasted salty and warm, but swallowing was too hard. I pushed the cup away.

"Please, love. I'm worried about you. I don't like worrying about you."

I knew those words, and it was cruel for my subconscious to parrot them back at me now, when he was no longer worried at all. I looked up, and there he was, perhaps even more perfect in my dream state than in real life. He was the sun. He'd always been the sun—shining and brilliant.

This was too much. I was hurting inside and out.

"I miss you," I told my sun. "I was so stupid. And now I've lost the light."

He didn't say he missed me back. He didn't say any of the things I would want from him. He told me, "Drink, Bliss. We'll talk when you are well."

I did as he asked because I was too tired to fight, too tired to make myself face the unreality. Slowly, I sipped, tipping my head back and letting the liquid slide down my throat so I didn't have to work so hard to swallow. Halfway through the cup, I could take no more. I pushed it away and he let me.

"Now you can sleep. Sleep, love."

I fell back against the pillows, but I was seized by something else . . . by fear. I feared losing this dream space between worlds where I hadn't ruined anything. Maybe Cade would arrive next, and Kelsey. And for a little while my life could be simple again.

Dream Garrick brushed a hand across my forehead. "I think your fever is almost gone. That's good. You should feel much better in the morning."

I frowned. "That means I'll have to call you soon."

"Call me?"

"To tell you that you might get sick too."

His head tilted sideways. Why didn't he understand?

"You don't think I already know?"

"Not you. You're not real."

"I'm not?"

"Real Garrick wouldn't be here." I curled into my pillow, wishing this dream would stop.

It wasn't nice anymore. It wasn't real. We weren't anything to each other . . . not anymore.

But Dream Garrick stayed there, his hand on my hair, and I let myself believe it for a little while longer.

24

At around four in the morning, I woke in a pool of sweat, my body stuck to the sheets and my face glued to the bed.

I guess the fever had definitely broken.

I placed my hands on the bed to push myself up, but my equilibrium must have been off. My bed felt uneven. I reached back, fumbling for the lamp and flicked the light on. Then, because I thought maybe I was seeing things, I flipped it off and on again. I pinched myself. I pinched *really* hard. But nothing changed.

Garrick was definitely asleep in my bed.

Shit.

Shit.

How much of my fever-induced dream was real? I felt safe assuming that my time as a bee was fiction, as well as a few mythological animals that I swore I'd seen. And that I hadn't really been living on the sun with aliens.

But Garrick was in my bed. He'd definitely been in my dreams, but it couldn't all be real. Sometimes he flew, much of the time he was naked. And there were a dozen more moments, some fuzzy, some very clear. Where was the line? What had really happened? Hell, was *this* even real? Maybe I was just dreaming that my fever broke. I was freaking out, and before I had the sense of mind to formulate a plan, I was already shaking him awake.

He was bleary-eyed and beautiful as he came to. I was struck for a moment by the fact that he was sleeping on my pillow.

He is in my bed. With me.

Sleeping.

We are sleeping together!

"You're awake." God, since when did groggy and gorgeous go so well together? Wide-eyed, I nodded, not having thought of what I'd say when I actually had him awake.

"How do you feel?"

That I could answer.

"Like shit. Everything hurts. My throat the worst."

He reached out and set a hand on my thigh. Like that was normal. Like we just set our hands on each other's thighs all the time.

"That's normal, I think," he said. The thigh thing? No, no . . . my throat. He continued. "Do you need anything?"

I shook my head. What the hell had happened while I was so out of it?

He sat up, and the sheet fell around his waist, revealing all of his upper body to my eyes. The sheet drooped around his hips, drawing my eyes to the muscles that disappeared down into his shorts. God. His hand went to my hair, my hair that fell lank and oily against my face, a stark contrast to how good he looked right now. He didn't seem to care.

Again, what the hell was happening?

"I'm glad you're okay," he said.

I nodded. Nodding was all I knew how to do, all I understood. Nodding, at least, still made sense.

"You should go back to sleep. You still need to rest. Unless you're hungry?"

I shook my head.

"Then sleep."

He nudged me slightly, and I lowered my body slowly, certain that the minute my head hit the pillow this alternate universe would cease to exist.

It didn't.

He pushed back the covers and then slipped out of the bed.

"You're leaving?" I asked.

He stopped, and in quick succession I saw him realize where we were and how little he was wearing. He hesitated, unsure. It was such a strange emotion, one I'd rarely seen him wear. "Do you want me to?" I wanted to pause the moment, study it, break down the second where this bold boy had been filled with doubt. Of course I didn't want him to leave! I never wanted him to leave!

I shook my head. Glad that fatigue kept me calm, somewhat.

He smiled so wide I forgot that the doubt ever existed. "Then I'm not leaving. I'm just going to get some water. Go to sleep."

He left, and I turned on my side, reeling. I could hear the faucet turn on and off. I tried to imagine what he was doing. The floor wasn't creaking, so he wasn't walking back. Was he just standing at the sink drinking? Or was there no creaking because my delusion had ended and he wasn't coming back? Had the floor creaked on his way to the sink? I couldn't remember. I started to panic. Maybe I needed to get up, go after him. Make sure he was real.

Then my bed dipped, and I felt heat behind me, and an arm wrapped around my waist. I stiffened first, and then relaxed so suddenly that I practically fell into him. He was so warm, I felt like I was feverish all over again.

He pushed my hair up and onto the pillow, so that my neck was uncovered. Then I felt something, the tip of his nose perhaps, grazing softly against my skin, and the puff of his breath.

"Garrick?"

His arm tightened, his body curved around mine, even our thighs pressed together.

"Tomorrow, Bliss. Sleep now."

Sleep? The idea seemed impossible, but as his breath steadied and I grew used to his touch, I realized I *was* still tired. I wanted to analyze what had happened, what I remembered and what I didn't, but sleep did seem more important.

Garrick was right. It could wait until the next day. He would be there. He said he wasn't leaving. But just in case, I placed one of my hands over his hand resting against my stomach. I had thought he was already asleep, but he was awake enough to respond, lacing our fingers together.

When I felt certain, both that he was real and that he wasn't leaving, when my doubt was gone, I slept.

I woke several hours later. Light was pouring in through my high windows, and my skin was slick with sweat. For a moment, I thought I had a fever again. I sat up, and Garrick's arm fell from my waist. He groaned.

His brow was furrowed, and beads of sweat dotted his face. I pressed my hand against his forehead, and sure enough, he was burning up. He looked awful, but I imagined that I looked even worse. My skin and clothes were damp with sweat, both his and mine. It felt like grime and sickness was slathered over my skin.

Carefully, I shifted out of Garrick's reach and planted my feet on the cool hardwood floor. Standing hurt all the way to my bones, like they'd been broken and set in the wrong way, and now I had to rebreak them to set them right. Each step felt like a nail gun shooting at my heels, my knees, my hips. It took a hand on the wall just to keep myself upright. And my journey to the bathroom comprised thirty slow, shuffling steps instead of the usual ten. When I got there, I was short of breath and ready for another nap.

In my pain-addled mind, it seemed very important to be clean first. I turned on the shower, leaving it on the cool side of the spectrum instead of automatically pushing it to hot as usual. I shucked off my clothes, lamenting each time I got off one piece only to discover another layer beneath. When I got to my bra, I nearly gave up completely.

Finally I was free, but I no longer had the energy to stand

for the shower I wanted. Like a child just learning to walk, I crawled into the tub, lying back and letting the water pelt my skin. My stomach especially felt so sensitive that each drop stung on impact, like someone was dropping tiny little missiles from above. But even so, it was cool and lovely, and I melted into the sensation.

For a long time I lay there, falling in and out of sleep. When my breath settled and the ache in my muscles eased, I pushed myself up, letting the water soak my hair and run down my face.

Shampoo became the villain of my story, stinging my eyes and exhausting me as I tried to rub it in and rinse it out. It felt like hours before the water ran clear enough to be able to open my eyes without them burning. And then I couldn't convince myself to do it again with conditioner.

I turned off the water and lay back, feeling the water drain beneath me. The longer my eyes stayed closed the heavier my body became. The little pools of liquid on my skin dried slowly, and it felt good to be empty, to be still for a moment.

Then I remembered Garrick and knew I had been selfish long enough.

The wall of the tub might as well have been a battlement. It took all of my strength to climb over it. Clothing was completely out of the question. I wrapped my hair in a towel and my body in a robe. I grabbed a few washcloths, soaking them with cool water, wringing them out so they wouldn't drip.

I felt a little more alive now, and I managed to walk without groping at the wall. The pain was there, in the back of my mind, with every step, but it was manageable. Even so, it was a relief to sink down beside Garrick on my bed.

I stripped the blankets back, and he shifted but didn't wake. I placed one of the damp cloths across his forehead, and another I unfolded and laid across his chest. I used the last to dab at his arms and legs. Even that became too difficult, though, so I rolled the last cloth up and slipped it beneath his neck.

Then I lay down beside him and slept.

The next time we woke together. His fever was still going, but I convinced him to drink some water. It wasn't until I took a drink myself that I realized how thirsty I was. I helped him drink a full glass and then gulped down two of my own. I had enough energy to shuck my thick robe and replace it with loose pajamas. I placed a new damp cloth on Garrick's forehead, and he sighed.

"Thank you," he mumbled.

I wasn't sure how coherent he was. He definitely knew I was there, as he'd called out my name a few times since he woke. And he knew he was sick, but I didn't know how much he knew beyond that.

"You're welcome. But to be fair, you did take care of me first."

His eyes were closed, but he smiled. "You're better at it."

"It doesn't matter," I said. "It was just nice not to be alone."

He tried to shift onto his side to face me, but ended up just reaching with his arms, his body still flat. I wrapped an arm around his chest and pulled him around. His arms went around me and pulled too, so that he ended up on his side and much closer to me.

When he was settled, he breathed out, exhausted by the little movement. He said, "I'm sorry."

"For what?"

For needing help? He seemed much stronger and better off than I had been.

"For leaving you alone at all. For getting between you and Cade. For being too stubborn to tell you I missed you. I'm sorry."

I was confused, the pieces of the puzzle not quite fitting. But I heard what mattered—he was sorry and I was sorry too. And my brain was too fuzzy to remember all the details of why this shouldn't be happening. I pulled him to me, and his head fell into the crook of my neck. I breathed deeply for what felt like the first time in months. I wanted to ask him about the phone call, about our fight, about everything. But he was still murmuring "sorry," again and again into my neck, and it didn't really matter.

I held him tighter, and together we weathered the sickness and slept.

25

We passed days in this manner, wrapped up in each other, in and out of sleep, eating and showering when we felt like we could. It was strange to think of sickness as an oasis, but that's what it was. When our physical needs triumphed over our brains, we didn't need to talk, not about our relationship or what had broken it. We didn't need to work anything out or explain ourselves. I didn't even have to worry about being a virgin or the idea of having sex with him.

We cradled each other and found healing in the quiet, beneath my covers, away from the world. By Saturday we were well enough to spend more time out of bed, to eat real food, to watch TV . . . to talk.

We lay on the couch, my back to his chest, his arm snug around me. We were supposed to be watching TV, but his forehead was pressed into my neck, and I was grilling him on the first days of my sickness.

"What did Eric say when you called him?"

"He wasn't upset, if that's what you're asking. Half the cast is sick now, I think."

Great. Our show was going to suck balls if we were all exhausted all the time. We could call it an experimental piece—*Phaedra Lethargic.*

I asked another question. "What did he say about you taking care of me?"

His forehead lifted off my neck. "He doesn't know. He told me to get you in bed, and you'd be fine. He suggested that I use your phone to call your mum."

That would have been horrific. Knowing my mother, she would have asked him when he planned to pop the question right after she found out his name.

"But you stayed."

"I couldn't just leave you. I told Eric I wasn't feeling well either, and I stayed with you."

"But why?"

"Do you really have to ask?"

"I do." I'd heard him all those weeks ago on that phone call, heard him say that he didn't care, that I was just inconvenient. Whatever the reason he'd stayed, I needed to hear it.

He said, "Well, then, if we're doing this, I'm doing it the right way."

He tried to sit up behind me, but our position on the couch was snug, and we were both still a little out of sorts, so we ended up tangled, him practically on top of me. I was still stuck on my side, squished beneath him. He tried to wiggle off of me, but his movements were reminiscent of a turtle on its back. Finally, he gave up and lifted up just enough so that I could turn onto my back, and then he lowered himself more gently on top of me.

Despite the fact that we'd slept in the same bed for a week, this was still intimate, still exciting, still terrifying. He held himself up on his elbows as much he could, but he was weak, so his weight still pressed into me.

I liked it.

"What was I saying again?" he asked. "Oh, right, that I might be falling in love with you."

I blinked. Then blinked again.

I blink-blink-blinked my way through a multitude of emotions in mere seconds—shock, disbelief, excitement, fear, lust, uncertainty, and settled on something . . . something too big for a name. There was a galaxy inside of me— complex and infinite and miraculous and fragile. And at the center was my sun. Garrick. Love. The two were like synonyms to me now. He was falling in love with me? *With me?*

A brush of his hand brought me out of that universe and back into the moment. "You could drive a man crazy with that kind of silence."

"I love you too," I said. Then I remembered that he hadn't *quite* said those three words. He'd said he was *falling* in love with me. And there had been a maybe in there. Shit. "I mean . . . what I should have said was that I feel the same. I'm just falling too. Because already being in love with you is too fast. That would be crazy. It's too much, right? It's too much.

It's too fast. So . . . I'm not in love with you. I'm not. Not that you're not lovable, it's just, there's a difference between falling in love and *being* in love. And we are the first, not the second, not yet. So I too may be falling in love with you. That's what I meant to say. That's *all* I meant to say." I was falling apart. His eyes were soft and unchanging and gave nothing away, so I kept devolving into incoherency. Finally, he kissed me, quickly, but it felt like a punctuation, like I could finally stop *talking*.

I sighed. "You're supposed to do that *before* I start crazy-talking."

He laughed and kissed me again, a little longer this time.

"I like your crazy talk. Better yet, I love your crazy talk. It's settled. I'm no longer falling. I am definitely in love with you. That's not too much, is it?" His grin was blinding and so mocking that I gave him a swift pinch to the arm.

He didn't even have the decency to look pained. He just kissed me, pressing all of his weight into me, and it was the best kind of "too much."

I'd always thought too much, was too much in my head, as Eric said. But since I'd met Garrick, I'd had an embarrassing tendency to stop thinking completely. The things that came out of my mouth as a response were almost always embarrassing, but sometimes they worked out. Sometimes saying the first thing that came to mind went well. Sometimes simple and honest worked the best.

I *hoped* this was one of those moments.

"I'm a virgin," I told him. "That's why I ran away the night we met. I didn't have a cat. I wasn't with Cade. I was just afraid."

He paused mid-kiss on my neck. Then slowly—like shifting-of-tectonic-plates slowly—he lifted his head. He stared at me, into me, through me. I resisted the urge to hide my face, to run away screaming, to make up ridiculous excuses involving some other kind of animal. I whispered, "You could drive a girl crazy with that kind of silence."

His reaction was small—just the skin between his eyebrows pinching together.

"Let me get this straight . . . you didn't have a cat? Did you *get a cat* just so that you wouldn't have to tell me you were a virgin?"

I pressed my lips together to keep them from trembling. I nodded. The look on his face was somewhere between shock and amusement. He was flabbergasted. That was the best word. His flabber had been thoroughly gasted.

"You said you loved my craziness," I reminded him.

"I do. I love you. It's just . . . honestly? I'm relieved."

"You're relieved that I'm a virgin? What did you think I was—a hoe-bag?"

"I would never think you were a hoe-bag." Was it completely inappropriate to find the way he said "hoe-bag" adorable? "But I knew you were hiding something. I was worried there was some other reason you didn't want to be with me. I've been paranoid about it for months."

"You've been paranoid? I heard that phone call where you said I was an inconvenience. You were planning to change jobs because of me. I was petrified if I ever looked at you too long or gave away how much I missed you that you'd pack up and leave."

"What are you talking about? I was never planning to leave."

"I heard you. That day I came by the office. You were on the phone with someone back in Philadelphia, and you said you were over us, that it had just been an inconvenience—"

He held a hand to my lips, "Bliss, now I *will* stop your crazy talk. While our situation is anything but convenient, *you* have never been an inconvenience to me. And I wouldn't have left even if they fired me. I was far too enamored with you." I resisted the urge to correct his use of the past tense. He *is* enamored with me. He loves me. God, that felt good. So good, I might get it tattooed somewhere on my body.

He blew out a breath, and the blond strands on his forehead danced in response. "The phone call was actually about something that happened before I left Philadelphia. It's part of *why* I'd left Philadelphia."

I remembered that, on that long-ago day when I'd asked why he left Philly, he'd changed the subject rather effectively by kissing me. I hadn't cared then. Maybe if I had, things would have happened differently. He shifted off of me, moving once more to his side, next to me. He barely looked at me as he spoke, "I had a friend, Jenna. Our relationship was a lot like your relationship with Cade. We became friends during graduate school, and even though I knew it was a bad idea, we tried to be more. I cared about her, but as a friend and nothing more. When I ended the relationship—well, it was a disaster. We were working on a show together. We did a lot of work at the same theatres, and much like the early Phaedra rehearsals, we ruined everything we did together. As a result,

I was having trouble finding work, and most of our friends had taken Jen's side, so when Eric offered me an out, I ran. I was so ashamed at first. I'd quit. I'd given up. And I'd lost a good friend in the process. The phone call you heard was about Jen. That's what I was over. And that's why I came down so hard on you and Cade. I was terrified you would go to him, even though I knew you were just friends. I was scared you'd make the same mistake I did. I'm sorry. I handled this all so badly. If I had told you when you asked, you might have understood—"

It was my turn to stop him with a kiss. I turned onto my side and pulled him against me. I poured every misplaced emotion into that kiss—the uncertainty I'd felt about his feelings, the fear of my virginity, the remorse over all the time we'd wasted. I let go of all those things, sent them off with a kiss.

"I understand now," I told him. "That's what matters."

"I love you," he said. I would never get tired of that.

"I love you too."

He said, "Can you say that one more time? So that I can be sure it's not the sickness addling my brain?"

I kissed him, softly. In our current state, softly was about all we could manage.

"I love you, Garrick."

It was shocking how *not* scared I was.

Not anymore.

26

A gold necklace sat weighted and heavy around my neck. My hair was piled in curls and jewels, and my dress, though sweeping and simple, was heavy and lush. I sat staring in the dressing room mirror as the makeup designer put finishing touches on my hair and I finished putting on my stage makeup. It was opening night, and despite my heavy costume and jewelry, I felt like I was going to float away.

Excitement rushed faster than blood through my veins.

We were here. Finally. The widespread sickness had delayed the opening by a week, but even so, I thought the show was good. Really good. And I wasn't alone.

Kelsey came careening into the room, looking drop-dead gorgeous as Aphrodite. "I know, I know. You don't have to stare. I know how amazing I look."

I smiled, just feeling glad to have her back. She'd been the only one of my close friends to evade the dreaded mono, which was incredibly cruel considering that spin the bottle had been her idea.

She'd shown up on the last day of spring break to demand that we "stop being prissy girls and make up already," only to find Garrick and me curled up in bed together. She'd pieced together pretty quickly why I hadn't wanted to go out dancing that night, and with a wide grin she backed out of my room saying, "Don't mind me. I didn't see anything. My lips are sealed." At first, Garrick had totally freaked, but since then she had definitely become an ally.

She smiled at Megan, the designer finishing my hair, and said, "Looks great, Meg! You're fantastic! I think Alyssa needed you for something, though, so you might want to finish up fast."

Megan nodded, spraying the final product with half a can of hairspray before fleeing the dressing room.

Kelsey threw herself into a chair beside me. "You're welcome. And first, you look gorgeous. I'm a little envious. Shouldn't Aphrodite have a better dress?"

I rolled my eyes.

"All right, okay. Never mind. Secondly, you're going to be amazing tonight. Seriously. Like, give-her-a-Tony-now amazing. Third, break a leg." She leaned in and licked the side of my face, some weird pre-show tradition she'd had for as long as I'd known her. "And lastly, there's someone else waiting outside to wish you a good show. You've got five minutes until warm-up. I can promise you privacy for three, so you better take advantage while you can."

She placed a quick air-kiss on my cheek, then skipped toward the door and shut it behind her once Garrick had slipped inside.

"Hi," he said.

"Hey."

He stepped into the room as I stood in the middle of it. It was disconcerting to see myself in the dozens of mirrors all around the room, so I focused on him, which wasn't hard. He looked gorgeous as always.

"You look . . ." he paused, taking in my elaborate, midnight blue costume.

"If you say cute, I will skin you alive."

He smiled and pulled me to him. Careful not to smudge my makeup, he placed a kiss on my neck instead, then dipped and dropped a kiss over my heart, just above the line of my gown. I clutched his shoulders, feeling lightheaded at his touch.

He said, "I was going to say you looked unbelievably sexy. I'm glad you're not my stepmum."

I laughed. "I'm not sure being your student is much better."

He dragged his lips up my neck and then brought our faces close together. His blue eyes, dark and decadent, almost matched the color of my dress.

"One month," he said. We had one month until he was no longer my teacher and I was no longer a college student. One month until it didn't matter how we felt and who knew about it. One month until we planned to have sex.

It had seemed like a reasonable plan when we were holed up sick in my apartment. It gave me the time I needed to deal with my anxiety, and it held significance since we could no longer get in trouble. But the more he looked at me like *that,* like he was looking at me now, like he loved me, the less I cared about waiting.

"I wish I could really kiss you," he said, staring mournfully at my lips, which were full and red thanks to layers of stage makeup.

"Tonight," I told him. "After the party. My place?"

He leaned forward, at the last second swerving from my lips and kissing me in that spot below my ear that he *knew* made my knees go weak.

"It can't come soon enough. 'I feel all the furies of desire.'" He quoted one of my lines from the show back at me, and that reminded me that we were probably near the end of our time.

"You should probably go before everyone else gets back. Tell Kelsey 'thank you' on your way out?"

"Oh, I will. Best thing that ever happened to me . . . that girl finding out about us."

I turned back to the mirror, making sure my makeup and hair still looked perfect. "I'm going to pretend you didn't just say my best friend was the best thing to ever happen to you."

Even though he was supposed to be leaving, he raced back to my side and circled his arms around me from behind. He kissed my neck one last time and said, "I love you." I looked at him through the mirror. We looked good together—he in a suit, me in an elaborate Grecian gown. It was still kind of unbelievable, this thing we had. "I love you too," I said.

I stayed staring in the mirror after he left, thinking that I looked different. Not just the costume and hair and makeup—me. I looked . . . happy.

I heard Alyssa call for warm-up, and I took a deep breath, trying to calm my sprinting heart.

Today was a big day.

Our first *Phaedra* performance.

My last opening night here ever.

And if I got my way, the night I lost my virginity.

There are moments in theatre when everything comes together exactly how it is supposed to happen. The costumes and set are perfect, the audience rapt and engaged, and the acting effortless.

This night was one of those nights.

Every actor was on fire.

And I . . . I lived another life in those two hours onstage. I lived the shame. It was a familiar emotion to me. I lived the hope when word came of my husband's death. I dreamed that maybe . . . maybe Hippolytus could be mine. I felt the horror when my affections weren't returned and when I learned that my husband wasn't dead after all. I experienced the pain of remorse when Hippolytus was killed based on my false accusations. And then finally, I felt the acceptance, the release, of admitting my crimes, and it was almost as if I could feel the poison Phaedra took coursing through my blood, reaching for my heart. It wasn't until I had crumpled on the floor, Theseus's last lines had been delivered, and the lights had dimmed that I really came out of it.

The clapping started in the dark, and my breath caught

in my throat. I fought back the tears that came with experiencing something as perfect and powerful as the performance I'd just had. That was what theatre was about—that kind of experience. We would never be able to re-create it again. Only the people who were here this night would ever know what this show was like.

Theatre is once in a lifetime . . . every time.

It was like the stars aligned, because suddenly so many more things about my life became obvious. Things that had eluded me until now were laid plain in my mind. Everything made sense, and I couldn't wait to see Garrick. Backstage was in an uproar when we left the stage after our final bows. Friends and family lined the halls between the stage door and the dressing rooms. Eric was there, smiling at us, proud of the show he'd put together. I hugged him first, so grateful that he had given me this chance and hadn't dumped me that first week when I was doing terrible.

"Best work I've ever seen you do, Bliss. You should be proud."

I was, God I was. My face felt split open by my smile.

Garrick was behind him, and even though it was risky, I hugged him too. He didn't hold me long, just long enough to whisper "Brilliant" in my ear.

Then I lost myself in the crowd.

I was slick with sweat, and my dress felt as heavy as another person hanging on me, but I relished the hugs and congratulations that poured over me.

And when I was back in the dressing room . . .

. . . I danced.

We all danced. Kelsey flipped on her iPod, and we celebrated as we peeled off the layers of our costumes. Our dressing room was filled with flowers, which helped to mask the sweat. When we'd put away our things, donned real clothes, removed our stage makeup, and reapplied real makeup, we moved the party elsewhere. We were heading to SideBar, the only bar close to campus that allowed people under twenty-one, a must when the whole cast was going.

I was surprised to find Cade waiting outside the dressing room when we exited. He stepped up beside me. "Hey, can I give you a ride to SideBar?"

That was surprising, but certainly welcome.

I told him, "That would be great, but I was planning on leaving early. I'm pretty tired."

"Oh," he nodded. "Well, do you mind if I ride with you, and I'll just find another ride home after?"

"Sure, that's fine with me."

We walked to my car in silence, and I jangled my keys to fill the space with noise. I started the car and immediately turned down the radio. "So, what's up, Cade?"

He fidgeted with his seat belt. Nervous. He didn't answer my question but instead asked, "How are things with Garrick?"

Frowning, I pulled out of the parking lot, watching him from the corner of my eye. "Why?"

"I'm sorry. Is that weird? I didn't mean for it to be weird, I was just trying to be friendly." He looked so uncomfortable. How had we been reduced to this?

I said, "It's not weird, Cade. I'm sorry. I'm just . . . a little cautious is all. Things are great actually."

He nodded, "Good. That's good."

After spending so much time with Garrick, I'd forgotten what it was like to deal with guys who didn't just say what they were thinking.

"Just tell me what you want to talk about, Cade. Whatever it is, it's fine."

He took a deep breath. He was still nervous, but he was no longer fidgeting. "I have a question, but I'm pretty sure it's prying, and I just don't want to cross any lines."

"Cade, I know things have been difficult. But I still consider you one of my best friends. I want you to be one of my best friends again. Ask me anything."

"Are you guys staying together after we graduate?"

My gut reaction was to say, "Yes." Even though Garrick and I hadn't really talked about it, not in so many words. We'd implied it, sure, with the whole "one month" thing, but we hadn't really had that conversation for real.

"Are you staying here? Or moving to Philly? Or somewhere else?"

I pulled into the parking lot, using the need to search for a space as an excuse to collect my thoughts. That was definitely not a conversation we'd had, no matter how much I had thought about it.

"Why do you ask?"

He ruffled his hair, and I resisted the urge to say, "Just spit it out already!"

"Well . . . I applied to a grad school a few months ago before . . . well . . . before everything. And I hadn't really thought I would go, but I got in, and now I'm thinking I might actually like it."

"Really? That's great, Cade!"

"It's Temple, in Philly."

"Oh." That was the school where Garrick had studied.

"And I just wasn't sure if the two of you were going to be in Philly, and if you thought it would be weird for me to be there too. And if it's not, I thought maybe we could still . . . you know, hang out. If that's cool with Garrick."

An image started to form in my mind of what that life might be like. It was a pretty great thought.

"I don't know if we'll be in Philly or not. But if we are . . . no, it won't be weird. And yes, we'll hang out. And Garrick can be cool or not cool with it; he doesn't decide what I do. I meant what I said, Cade. I really do want us to be friends again."

He smiled, relaxed in his seat finally. "Me too."

27

Cade wasn't the only one thinking about the future. At SideBar we did our fair share of celebrating and drinking and eating, but the talk soon turned sentimental. We shared memories of our first shows, classes we'd had together, parties that had gone horribly wrong. Rusty suggested that we could have another makeout party, and he was pelted with napkins and bits of paper and even a hot roll.

Just like with theatre—life sometimes has perfect moments when the stars all align and you're exactly where you want to be with great people, doing exactly what you want to do.

Leaving college seemed impossible.

I had never been happier than I'd been during the four years I'd spent there. I looked around the table as people laughed and screamed (we only had one volume—really loud). These people were my family. They understood me and knew me in ways that no one else did.

I couldn't imagine my life without them.

"Uh-oh! Tears alert!" Kelsey cried. "Bliss is getting weepy!"

I wiped at my eyes, and embarrassingly, she was right.

"Shut up! I just love you guys, okay?"

Kelsey's arms enfolded me first, then Rusty, then Cade, and then I lost count.

Rusty said, "Stop acting like we don't have a month left together. I don't know about you guys, but I have one hell of a college bucket list that I need you guys to help me fulfill. Starting with getting super-drunk on my last opening night. So let's get started."

I ate and drank, just listening to the stories and conversations around me, soaking it all up. Life was good, and if I had my way, it was about to get even better.

It was harder than I thought it would be to excuse myself after dinner was over. Not because I was nervous about what I planned to do that night—I actually felt good about that—but because I didn't want to leave my friends.

It's a funny thing to miss people before you've even left them, but that's what I was feeling now.

A little bit of melancholy stayed with me all the way out of the bar and into my car. But it didn't take long for it to disappear in light of where I was heading. I didn't text Garrick when I was on my way, like I'd told him I would, because I wanted some time to get things ready.

I took a quick shower and then left my hair loose to dry curly, because Garrick liked it that way. It made me think of that night at the club, and my heart beat faster just at the memory.

I found the Victoria's Secret bag in the back of my closet that held the lingerie I'd bought specifically with this night in mind. I slipped it on, trying to imagine again exactly what Garrick might think or feel when he saw me.

Looking in the mirror, I felt sexy, like he'd always said I was. I slipped back on the dress I'd worn after the show, not wanting to give anything away just yet. I tidied up my room, made sure there were condoms in the bedside table, and then took a seat on my bed.

I was doing this.

I was *really* doing this.

I was going to have sex with Garrick . . . tonight.

Something bubbled up in my chest. At first I thought it was nerves, but then I recognized it. It was the same kind of feeling I'd had when I first found out I'd been cast as Phaedra, and then again when the show had gone so well. It was something beyond excitement, something better.

Because I could, I hopped up on my bed, and jumped. It felt good, so I did it again. I flailed my arms because it seemed like the right thing to do, and then I covered my face with my hands and let out the quietest scream I could manage.

"What are you doing?"

Garrick was at the foot of my bed, an amused grin unfurled on his face. I squeaked and plopped back onto the bed.

"What are you doing here?" I asked.

"I saw your car outside, so I came over. I didn't realize you'd already started the party without me. I take it you're excited about how the show went tonight?"

I climbed off the bed as gracefully as I could (meaning with zero grace at all). I should have expected something like this. It seemed I was incapable of having an intimate moment with Garrick without doing something supremely embarrassing. At least this time it happened at the beginning.

"The show was great, but I'm glad to be home." I put a hand on his chest, and he wrapped his arms around me in a hug.

"You were great tonight, and now I get to have you all to myself."

I hadn't really thought about the best way to approach what I wanted to do tonight. I'd thought about the lingerie and the condoms and the probable pain, but not so much the "Hey, I'm ready to have sex" talk.

I mean, he was a guy, so I doubted very much he'd care about how I told him, but still . . . I wanted it to be right.

"How was the celebration?" he asked.

"Good, really good. I'm going to miss everyone when we graduate. It's a little crazy to think that's only a month away."

"One month." He smiled and leaned down for a kiss.

I think he meant for the kiss to be quick, but I didn't really give him a choice in the matter. I looped my arms around his neck to keep him down at my level and pressed my lips more firmly against his. He hummed lightly, and the vibrations tingled my lips. His hand curled around my rib cage, and I wanted it higher, farther in. I wanted him touching me everywhere.

When he was taking too long, I opened my mouth and traced the seam of his lips with my tongue. He let me in, and the taste of him was as addicting as always. With each brush of his tongue against mine, I felt more certain.

I pulled my arms down from his neck and slipped a hand underneath his shirt, pressing my fingertips into his back. His hands remained in safe places, my ribs and my neck, but I felt them twitch and tighten slightly at the skin-to-skin contact.

He kept kissing me . . . slowly, safely.

I slipped my other hand beneath his shirt, feeling the ridges of his abs, up to his chest. I hoped he would take the hint and move his own hand accordingly.

He didn't.

Frustrated, I shifted him slightly until my bed pressed at the back of his knees and then I pushed. He sank onto the bed, and I wasted no time climbing onto his lap, pressing against him in much the same way I had that first night we'd almost had sex.

"Bliss," he whispered. It was almost a warning, but not quite there yet.

I should probably have told him what I wanted, but the way he was kissing me . . . or more aptly, the way he wasn't kissing me . . . made me feel unsure, desperate. He still wanted me. I told myself that. And I believed it. Mostly. I just needed a little more reassurance.

I pulled back and waited for his eyes to open, for him to watch me. When his eyes met mine, they were a bit too clear, too focused, for my liking. I reached down and grabbed the hem of my dress. He made a noise in his throat when I started pulling it up, but I didn't stop until I had it up and over my head. At first his eyes stayed resolutely on mine, but when I leaned forward, taking care to brush my chest against his, he looked down.

His intake of breath was exactly what I'd been looking for.

The strapless black bra was so tight that I had possibly the best cleavage I had ever or will ever have. And the panties, well, you could barely call them that.

"Bliss." This time there definitely was a warning tone. "You're overestimating my self-control."

"Oh, I'm pretty sure I estimated your control perfectly."

I leaned forward until I was pressed tightly against his hips. My lips hovered over his, waiting for him to kiss me. I was done being on the offensive. It was his turn to come to me.

As always, the anticipation alone was enough to do me in. His gaze darted between my eyes and my mouth, and now that I was down to only lingerie, his hands met my skin no matter where he put them. One was currently scalding my lower back, and the other was fisted in my hair. I rocked my hips against him, and his hand in my hair tightened.

"Bliss." His response was choked, like he was in pain.

I smiled. This was kind of fun.

"Garrick," I returned, eyes wide and as innocent as I could make them.

"This is the opposite of slow."

I exhaled, swaying forward so that my bottom lip barely grazed his. I rubbed against him, grinding at the slowest pace I could. I said, "I think we've gone slow enough."

The arm at my back pulled me in more, until my chest pressed against his. He still had a shirt on. I wanted it gone.

"What does that mean?" Ah, there was that look I loved—dark, a bit unfocused.

"It means," I said as my hands found the bottom of his shirt, "that I'm done going slow."

I pulled, and his arms followed automatically, allowing me to pull the shirt over his head before his hands went right back into their previous positions. Our chests met, skin sliding against skin, and he groaned. He said, "I'm going to need you to be very clear about what you're saying right now, Bliss."

All right, it was time to just say it. And no euphemisms like beast with two backs or horizontal tango or anything ridiculous. Sex. If I was going to have it, I could sure as hell say it. I leaned in and kissed him for courage. To hell with making him come to me. That took too long. When I pulled back, his lips tried to follow. I appeased him with another quick kiss and said, "Make love to me?"

Everything about him tensed—his hands on me, his gorgeous face, and his body beneath mine.

"Bliss, you don't have to do anything you don't want to do for me."

"What about tonight has felt like I was being forced to do anything? In fact, I feel a little like I'm forcing you."

His lips crushed against mine—teeth and tongues and heat. It was just enough to make me shake with want, and then it was over.

Garrick was panting when he replied, "You're not forcing me to do anything. I just want you to be sure. You can say stop at anytime." His lips pulled wide. "You don't need to make up a new pet."

That grin . . . it was so infuriating and sexy at the same time.

I put my hands on his shoulders and pushed away, standing up. "If you're going to keep trying to talk me out of it. . . ."

I hadn't even taken one full step away before he'd grabbed me and spun me so that my back hit the mattress. My breath left my lungs in a rush, and the sight of him prowling above me made heat curl low in my belly.

"I wasn't trying to talk you out of anything. I was trying to be a gentleman."

Huh. He'd tried to pull the gentleman card that first night too. He was still hovering over me, and I looped my fingers into the belt loops on his jeans and tugged him down on top of me.

"Do me a favor? Be a gentleman tomorrow?"

I was fairly certain he said, "Yes, ma'am," but then he was kissing me, and I couldn't have cared less.

28

He kissed me hard, and long enough that I could taste more of him in my mouth than myself. I dug my fingernails into his shoulders because I had learned that every time I did he pressed his hips harder against mine.

If he wasn't careful, I would draw blood soon.

His hands smoothed up my sides, sending shivers across my skin when he passed the sensitive spots. And finally, one hand stole around my back, reaching for the clasp of my bra.

His lips left mine for the hollow of my neck. His chin, once again covered in scruff, grazed the top of my breasts.

I arched up toward him at the same moment that the snaps on my bra came undone. The cold air hardened my nipples into little buds, and I ached for him to touch me. He said once that we could own each other, and I wanted nothing more in that moment. Garrick kissed down between my breasts, his cheeks grazing slightly across the swells. I dug my fingernails in again, and his hips pressed down at the same moment that he took one breast into his hand and the other into his mouth. Something sparked beneath my skin, and I moaned, bucking up against him in response.

He rolled one nipple between his fingers, and the other he squeezed lightly between his teeth, and I could feel darkness creeping in on my vision.

Words streamed from my mouth, some familiar, some not.

The last of them were, "I love you."

He rose up off me with a grin. "If I'd known it was that easy to get you to admit how you feel, I would have done this a long time ago."

My brain was beyond responding with words. Instead, my hands found his belt. I unbuckled it and then flicked open the button to his jeans.

His cheeky smile was gone now.

Slowly, I pulled down his zipper, and the sound alone made a moan rise in my throat. I pushed his jeans and boxers down together. When he pulled back to shuck his pants off completely, I took the moment to slip my panties down and off and grab a condom from my drawer.

When he looked up, he froze for a second in shock, as if he just now realized how serious I was. He shook it off quickly and swooped in for a kiss.

"You know I love you, right?"

"I do," I told him. I don't think I could have done it if I didn't know that. That was what I'd needed. That was what made the fear and the nerves bearable.

He kissed me again, and his fingers found my entrance. He slipped two inside at the same time that his tongue met mine. He started slowly, then his kisses sped up along with his fingers. I squeezed his shoulders, my fingernails scraping lightly, and was rewarded with a crooking of his fingers inside me.

I moaned, breaking our kiss.

His lips returned again to my chest, placing featherlight kisses everywhere he could reach. I could feel a pressure building low in my core, and I pulled his head back up to mine. He pressed his forehead against mine, our lips touching, but not kissing, then his palm pressed down against me, and an explosion ignited beneath my skin. Like a string of fireworks, my world detonated into bursts of light and color.

The world was coming together and crumbling to pieces behind my closed eyes, and my mouth was still open in a silent scream. I felt his kiss below my ear, and I reached for him, wrapping my arms around his middle.

The length of him pressed against me, and my whole body shuddered in response.

"Are you sure?" he asked me again.

My brain didn't know how to play it cool at the moment, so I said, "Please, God, yes."

There was a pinching sensation, not pleasant, but the rest of my body was too relaxed to really think too much of the pain. He kissed me as he pushed inside, then broke off with a groan.

"Oh God, Bliss."

His whole body was tense above me. I could see the pronounced lines of his flexed muscles in his shoulders, in the arms braced on either side of me. I could feel it in the warm chest pressed against mine. I distracted myself from the pain by following those lines with my eyes and hands.

After a few moments, he took a deep breath and gazed at me. He soothed me first with his lips, and then with whispers of "love" and "beautiful" and "perfect."

He stilled completely once he was inside, crushing his lips against mine. My limbs felt a bit like Jell-O, so I just wrapped myself around him, holding him as tightly as I could.

He pulled out, just a little, before pushing back in.

I breathed out sharply, biting my lip against the twinge of pain.

Garrick's lips captured that bottom lip between his own, soothing, careful.

"Are you okay?" he asked.

I nodded, not sure I could speak.

"Do you need me to stop?"

I shook my head. That wasn't what I wanted at all. I wanted him to feel what I'd felt earlier. I wanted to hold him as he came apart in my arms.

He repeated the action, and this time it wasn't so much pain as discomfort.

"Keep going," I whispered.

Garrick burrowed his head into the curve of my neck, dragging his mouth over my pulse point as he pushed in and out again. The next time I was coherent enough to tip my hips upward to meet him halfway. His response was a groan that I felt all the way down to my toes.

His mouth memorized the skin of my neck and shoulders as we developed a rhythm between us. Something pushed and pulled inside of me, and each time our skin connected I felt the pressure build a little bit more. His hand cupped my breast, and I felt the pleasure snake down my middle to the place where our bodies met.

I wrapped my legs around his hips and pulled him farther into me. His rhythm stuttered for a moment, his eyes closed, and he was beautiful as he tried to hold himself together.

My whole world was expanding in the circle of his arms.

He started moving again after a moment, and this time he reached a hand between us. I'd worry about how he got to be so good at this later, but for now I was too busy reaping the benefits. I was so close, and every muscle in me was clenched tight. I dug my fingernails into his shoulder one final time, my favorite new trick, and his hips snapped forward.

"Bliss," he ground out.

I just wrapped my legs tighter against him and rolled my hips upward. His head dropped to my neck, his breath hot against my skin. He thrust forward again so hard that my whole body shifted and pleasure poured through my body so fast that my vision went spotty. His body stilled against mine, his face still pressed into my neck, his arms cradling me. I lifted his face to mine, watching as his eyes clenched shut and his mouth fell open, and his whole body shuddered over mine.

When his eyes opened, they were still dark, but focused on me. He pressed a kiss to my forehead, then each cheek, and finally my lips.

"I love you," we said together.

He slipped out of me, and I immediately reached for him, missing him, missing the way we fit together. He settled beside me and gathered me in his arms. I laid my head on his chest, where I could hear his heartbeat. It was just as fast as mine. He laced our fingers together and pressed his cheek into the top of my hair.

It was perfect.

I was full of perfect moments that day.

And I wasn't sure if what I said next would make it more so or ruin everything, but I'd found that not thinking too much worked well with Garrick. When my breathing calmed, I said, "I looked at apartments in Philadelphia."

"You did?"

I nodded, still unsure what he was thinking.

"I know we still haven't talked about this," I began. "But I've been doing some thinking, and I've decided I do want to focus on acting, not stage management, and since I can't afford New York, Philly seems like a pretty good place. I mean, I haven't made any final plans. I've only done some research. You know, looked at some theatres, upcoming auditions, apartments, and day jobs, that kind of thing. But if you don't think it's a good idea, I don't have to—"

"Stop right there, crazy talker."

This was an awful idea. I'd just ruined a great moment . . . like I always did. Seriously, I was going to invent some kind of machine to shock me or punch me in the face whenever I did shit like this. It would be like conditioning, and maybe eventually I'd learn to shut the hell up. His hand found my jaw and tilted my face up toward his. His thumb grazed my lip, and his eyes gazed into mine.

"I think you would love Philly," he told me.

The light was shining again in the form of his smile, and I relaxed into his arms.

"But don't worry about researching apartments. You can stay with me while you look for a place."

His face was carefully constructed—the lines smooth, his lips closed and resting somewhere close to a smile. I swallowed the lump in my throat and said, "Really?"

"And if you don't find a place you like, you can always decide to just stay with me permanently."

I reached up and brushed his hair back from his forehead so that I could see his eyes. "Are you asking me to move in with you? I can't tell. You're usually much more direct than that."

He smiled. "That was me attempting to ask you to move in with me without scaring you off. Did it work?"

I said, "I'm not scared."

And I meant it.

Epilogue

SIX MONTHS LATER

Garrick

My eyes were always drawn to Bliss during this scene. She was lovely and joyous, and it took all of my focus to keep from rushing to her. Our director had written her own adaptation of the classic *Pride and Prejudice,* and I doubted she'd approve of me adding my own adaptation wherein Bingley and Elizabeth end up together instead of Elizabeth marrying that surly Mr. Darcy. Bliss's eyes connected with mine, and even though I was supposed to be fawning over her character's sister, my character was the last thing on my mind. We moved into formation for a dance where we were constantly moving and spinning. Every time Bliss and I passed, our eyes would meet, our hands would brush, and I'd curse the casting director who didn't make me Darcy. I could be surly.

Immediately after the curtain call, I found her backstage and pulled her into my arms. "Garrick," she sighed into my embrace. The words vibrated against my chest, and I held her tighter.

I whispered into her ear, "You must allow me to tell you how ardently I admire and love you."

She laughed. "You say that every night after the show."

I pulled back, and my cheek slid against hers. The curls around her face tickled my forehead. "What can I say? I'm persistent."

She hummed, her lips pressed tightly together. "Persistent? I'd say unimaginative. You could at least get your own line."

I traced my fingers over her back. I could feel the stays in her corset. God, I'd love to see her in that. Only in that.

"You want something original, love?"

"I do. Tomorrow I expect the best line you've got, Mr. Taylor. But now I need to go get dressed."

She stepped away from me and moved toward the women's dressing room. She looked at me over her shoulder, and I felt that look go all the way through me. Several original things went through my mind, none of which I could say out loud. Her grin seemed to say that she knew exactly what I was thinking.

"Hurry," I said.

"Patience is a virtue, Mr. Taylor."

She knew that name made me mental. It made me feel

like her teacher again, which was infuriating and sexy as hell all at the same time. I went to say as much, but she'd already ducked into the dressing room.

I took a moment to breathe and clear my head.

Tonight . . . my plan started tonight. If I didn't, I'd probably end up blurting it out with no warning whatsoever. And with Bliss's tendency to panic, that was definitely not the way to go.

I changed out of my costume and hung it up for the maintenance crew as quickly as I could. Tomorrow was our day off, which meant it was laundry day. Good thing too, because my costume had definitely smelled better. A few castmates invited us out for drinks, but I begged off. I hoped Bliss did the same. I wanted her all to myself tonight.

I was dressed and waiting for Bliss in record time. When the first girl came out, she laughed and shook her head. She leaned back in and said, "Bliss, your boyfriend is practically salivating out here."

Boyfriend. I still wasn't quite used to that. Even after Bliss graduated, it was awkward when people saw us together. It was nice that we had something fresh in Philly. We didn't have to hide.

Every girl that exited gave me a knowing smile, but Bliss took her time, longer even than normal.

"Bliss!" I called through the door. "Are you trying to torture me?"

The door swung open again . . . it was another smirking actress, not Bliss. I sighed. The girl said, "I'm pretty sure she is."

I groaned and pressed my face into the wall. The door opened, and I didn't even bother looking.

"Go ahead, lover boy. I'm the last one left." I turned to find Alice, the older woman playing Mrs. Bennett. I smiled and reached for the door. Alice laughed, "Good luck!"

I didn't think anything of her reply until I walked into the dressing room.

Bloody hell.

Bliss was still wearing the corset, sitting in a chair staring at me through the mirror. Her breasts were pushed up and out, and her eyes were dark as she looked at me. She reached a hand up and started pulling bobby pins from her hair. It tumbled down around her shoulders, and my mouth went dry.

She was stunning.

"I thought I told you to be patient."

I forced my feet into motion and walked up behind her. I reached out and helped her with the pins. God, I loved her hair. I wrapped a curl around my finger and said, "I'm good at being patient. I'm just not good at staying away from you. Surely you know that by now."

She grinned and leaned her head back into my hands. "I think that's been obvious from the beginning."

I dropped my hands from her hair to her neck. I pressed down with my thumbs, massaging gently. Her eyes fluttered closed. Her lips parted. She had no idea how sexy she was. In that corset, she looked like a 1950s pinup girl.

I leaned down and pressed my lips to the curve of her shoulder. Somehow, despite being onstage under the heat of the lights for several hours, she still smelled divine. I dragged my mouth up her neck to that spot below her ear that drove her crazy.

She exhaled, like my kiss had pushed all the air out of her lungs. Her hand curled around the back of my head, pulling me closer. I smiled against her skin.

She said, "You've bewitched me."

I chuckled and traced a finger along the fine bone of her collarbones. I could map out the architecture of her body for days and never get bored.

"Body and soul?" I asked, quoting the play.

I opened my mouth and tasted her skin. It was almost as delicious as her groan that followed.

"Definitely," she said.

"Who is being unoriginal now?"

A knock at the door broke the spell between us. Benji, the stage manager, poked his head in the room. I turned so that I blocked Bliss and that corrupting corset.

"You guys about ready? I'm going to lock up."

"Sorry, Ben. We'll be out in just a sec." His expression was skeptical. "I promise. Two minutes."

As soon as he shut the door, Bliss stood. I had to close my eyes to keep from touching her. That corset . . . my God. I kept my eyes closed because that was the only way we'd make it out of here in two minutes. Even so, hearing her change clothes was torture. Every rustle of fabric and zipped zipper brought a vivid picture into my mind. Even though I couldn't see her, I could feel her presence, especially when she stepped in front of me.

Her hand curled around my neck, tilting my head down. I kept my eyes closed, but the heat of her breath caressed my face.

"Let's go home, *Mr. Taylor.*"

That name. I opened my eyes, and she was smirking. Two could play at that game. "Oh, Miss Edwards, I think that might deserve detention."

Her eyes narrowed.

"Or maybe a little punishment."

I got so much pleasure out of seeing the red rise to her cheeks.

"You wouldn't."

Rather than answering, I bent and hauled her over my shoulder. She squeaked and clutched at my back.

"Garrick!"

"Hush, Miss Edwards. I'm taking you home."

Benji was waiting impatiently by the backstage door. His frown deepened when he saw us. He said, "First, that was three minutes. I counted. Second, you two are disgusting. I feel like I'm watching some Lifetime movie."

I just laughed and told him good-night. Bliss only pouted at first, but when I kept her over my shoulder even as we left the building, she started to struggle.

"Okay, Garrick, you've made your point."

"I don't know what you're talking about. There's no point. I just like carrying you."

"Well, you've had your fun. Put me down."

I stopped for a moment and pretended to think. I took the opportunity to slide my hand up the back of her thigh.

I answered, "I, for one, think there's more fun to be had."

I set off again, and either Bliss was paralyzed or she was really interested in where my hand was going to go next because she didn't move again.

Until I started descending the stairs to the subway. Then she kicked her legs and gave a swift, warning pinch to my side. "Garrick, I refuse to let you carry me onto the subway. Down, now."

I could picture her face red with anger and suddenly wanted to see it. Flushed cheeks. Narrowed eyes. Pursed lips. When I got to the bottom of the stairs, I pulled, allowing her body to slide down mine. I kept my hands at her waist to slow her descent. The shifting of her body against mine was heavenly. She sucked in a breath, and when our faces were level, her eyes were not narrowed, but closed. Her lips weren't pursed, but her bottom lip was caught between her teeth in a way that made my mouth dry. Her cheeks were still flushed, but I had a feeling it wasn't about anger anymore.

"You did that on purpose," she said.

I laughed, and it came out raspy. She wasn't the only one affected by our closeness. "I definitely did that on purpose. I think we should make this a post-show ritual actually."

She shook her head and smiled, but she didn't say no. Even under the dim lights of the subway station, she was radiant. I still couldn't believe I could touch her. There was no one to pull us apart. Nothing to get us in trouble. I was tempted to announce my love for her to all the other commuters, but I didn't want to break this moment. I liked the quiet way she was looking at me, her eyes filled with more than just desire. She made me happy, and I hoped I was seeing the same in her right then. Suddenly, I was excited to get home and put my plan into action.

I buried my fingers in her hair and pulled her in for a

kiss. Her hands tightened on my shoulders, her fingernails pressing into my skin. I took my time tasting her mouth, losing myself as we waited for the train.

As soon as we arrived home, I told Bliss I was going to take a shower. Sundays were two-show days, so I certainly needed it. I let her go in first to brush her teeth. I waited for the water to turn on, then leapt into action. I found Hamlet's feathered cat toy (the only reason she would ever willingly get close to Bliss) and hid it underneath the bed. Then I went to the closet and found the suit coat pocket where I'd hidden the ring. I popped open the box to look at it one more time.

It wasn't much. I was only an actor, after all. But Bliss wasn't one to wear much jewelry anyway. It was simple and sparkling, and I hoped she would love it as much as I loved her. A popping sensation filled my gut like those silly candy rocks that Bliss loved.

What if I was pushing her too fast?

No. No, I'd thought this out. It was the best way. I opened the top drawer of the nightstand and slid the ring box toward the back. The water in the bathroom shut off, and I went back to the closet, shucking my shirt. I tossed it in the hamper at the same time Bliss walked in the room.

She came up behind me and placed a hand on my bare back. She pressed a small kiss on my shoulder and asked, "Get Hamlet for me before you shower?"

I smiled and nodded.

Bliss was so determined to make Hamlet like her that she played with the cat for at least half an hour before bed every night. Hamlet would stick around for as long as Bliss waved that feathered toy in the air, but the minute Bliss tried to touch her, she was gone.

I found Hamlet in the kitchen, hiding underneath the kitchen table. I reached a hand down, and she butted her head against my fingers, purring. I picked her up at the same time that Bliss asked, "Babe, have you seen the cat toy?"

I walked into the room and deposited Hamlet on the bed. She hunkered down and eyed Bliss with distrust.

"Where did you see it last?" I asked her.

"I thought I'd left it on the dresser, but I can't find it."

I petted Hamlet once to keep her calm, then placed a quick kiss on Bliss's cheek.

"I don't know, honey. Are you sure you didn't leave it somewhere else?"

She sighed and started looking in other spots around the room. I turned and hid my smile as I left. I nipped into the bathroom and turned the shower on. I waited a few seconds, then went back to the hallway.

"Bliss?" I called.

"Yeah?"

"Check the drawers of the nightstand! She was playing with it in the middle of the night, and I think I remember taking it away and sticking it in there."

"Okay!"

Through the open door, I watched her circle around the edge of the bed. I walked in place for a few seconds, letting my feet drop a little heavier than necessary, then opened and closed the door like I'd gone back inside the bathroom. Then I hid in the space between the back of the bedroom door and the wall where I could just see through the crack between the hinges. She pulled open the top drawer, and my heartbeat was like a bass drum. I don't know when it had started beating so hard, but now it was all that I could hear.

It wasn't like I was asking her to marry me now. I just knew Bliss—I knew she tended to panic. I was giving her a very big, very obvious hint so that she'd have time to adjust before I actually asked her. Then, in a few months, when I thought she'd gotten used to the idea, I'd ask her for real.

That was the plan anyway. It was supposed to be simple, but this felt . . . complicated. Suddenly, I thought of all the thousands of ways this could go wrong. What if she freaked out? What if she ran like she did our first night together? If she ran, would she go back to Texas? Or would she go to Cade, who lived in North Philly? He'd let her stay until she figured things out, and then what if something developed between them?

What if she just flat out told me no? Everything was good right now. Perfect actually. What if I was ruining it by pulling this stunt?

I was so caught up in my doomsday predictions that I didn't even see the moment when she found the box. I heard her open it, though, and I heard her exhale and say, "Oh, my God."

Where before my mouth had been dry, now I couldn't swallow fast enough. My hands were shaking against the door. She was just standing there with her back to me. I couldn't see her face. All I could see was her tense, straight spine. She swayed slightly.

What if she passed out? What if I'd scared her so much that she actually lost consciousness? I started to think of ways to explain it away.

I was keeping it for a friend?

It was a prop for a show?

It was . . . it was . . . shit, I didn't know.

I could just apologize. Tell her I knew it was too fast.

I waited for her to do something—scream, run, cry, faint. Anything would be better than her stillness. I should have just been honest with her. I wasn't good at things like this. I said what I was thinking—no plans, no manipulation.

Finally, when I thought my body would crumple under the stress alone, she turned. She faced the bed, and I only got her profile, but she was biting her lip. What did that mean? Was she just thinking? Thinking of a way to get out of it?

Then, slowly, like the sunrise peeking over the horizon, she smiled.

She snapped the box closed.

She didn't scream. She didn't run. She didn't faint.

There might have been a little crying.

But mostly . . . she danced.

She swayed and jumped and smiled the same way she had when the cast list was posted for *Phaedra*. She lost herself the same way she did after opening night, right before we made love for the first time.

Maybe I didn't have to wait a few months after all.

She said she wanted my best line tomorrow after the show, and now I knew what it was going to be.

ACKNOWLEDGMENTS

Writing this book was nothing short of a whirlwind. I got the idea, and it was different than anything else I'd written before. My sister encouraged me to write it, and then, in only a matter of weeks, I had a first draft. The journey of publication was similarly chaotic and wonderful. Through it all, I have quite a few people to thank.

First, I have to thank my mother, who instilled in me a love of books. Thank you for being my teacher and my friend. Thank you for proofreading pretty much everything I write. Thank you for always laughing at my jokes even if you don't get them. Thank you for always believing that I was gifted enough to make my dreams come true. To my dad, I know my choices stress you out. We've argued about a lot of them, but you are always there when I need you. Thank you for caring so much that you lose sleep at night and for checking my Amazon rankings even more frequently than I do. To my sisters, thank you for loving books with me, for listening to me blather on about my ideas, for being enthusiastic about my work when I am unsure, and for putting up with the windmill. I love you.

Thank you to Lindsay and Michelle, my first readers. I don't think I would have ever finished this book if you two hadn't loved it as much as you did. Thanks to Ana for being my cheerleader. You know I'll always return the favor. And thank you to Heather for answering my plethora of questions. Thanks to Bethany, Lindsay, Joey, Patrick, Kristin, Zach, Marylee, Shelly, Sam, Justin, and all my other theatre friends who provided ample inspiration, made me believe awkward could be cool, and have been so supportive of me.

A *huge* thanks goes to Suzie Townsend, my dream agent, who read my book even though she'd sworn off New Adult. I couldn't have asked for a better advocate. Thanks also to Kathleen, Pouya, Joanna, and all the New Leaf ninjas! You are all incredible, and I'm so happy that you are all on my side (and that we saw Tyra together). Thanks to Amanda and Harper-Collins for loving this book as much as I do. Thank you to both Georgia McBride and Kevan Lyon for being amazing at your jobs and two of the nicest people in the world.

And last, but certainly not least, thanks to all those who read, reviewed, and spread the word via blogs, Twitter, Facebook, Tumblr, Instagram, etc. This book would not be where it is without you all. I owe you all my gratitude.

ABOUT THE AUTHOR

Cora Carmack is a twentysomething writer who likes to write about twentysomething characters. She's done a multitude of things in her life—retail, theatre, teaching, and writing. She loves theatre, travel, and anything that makes her laugh. She enjoys placing her characters in the most awkward situations possible and then trying to help them get a boyfriend out of it. Awkward people need love too.

Follow her on twitter @CoraCarmack

Visit her blog at http://coracarmack.blogspot.com for updates about future awkward romances!

If you loved Bliss and Garrick's story, don't
miss out on Cade's turn at love . . .

FAKING IT

BY CORA CARMACK

Coming soon from Ebury Press

Grad school isn't what Cade Winston thought it would be.
He's barely doing any acting and he still sees his best friend,
the girl who broke his heart, with another guy on a regular
basis.

When Mackenzie "Max" Miller sits across from him at a
coffee shop, it's like she blew into his life with the force of a
hurricane. She's the complete opposite of any girl he's ever
dated—brightly dyed hair, tattoos, a piercing, and a request.
She wants him to pretend to be her wholesome, boy-next-
door boyfriend for an hour so that her parents don't meet the
real guy she's dating. Maybe it's the weeks without acting or
maybe he's lost his mind, but he agrees to play the part.

Only neither of them planned for Cade's acting and
charm to win her parents over so completely. Now they're in-
sisting he come visit for the Christmas holidays. Max still has
a boyfriend, Cade is still heartbroken, and neither of them is
the other's type. But the more they fake it, the more it begins
to feel real.

1

Cade

You would think I'd be used to it by now. That it wouldn't feel like a rusty eggbeater to the heart every time I saw them together.

You would think I would stop subjecting myself to the torture of seeing the girl I love with another guy.

You would be wrong on all counts.

A Nor'easter had just blown through, so the Philadelphia air was crisp. Day-old snow still crunched beneath my boots. The sound seemed unusually loud, like I was walking toward the gallows instead of coffee with friends.

Friends. I gave one of those funny-it's-not-actually-funny laughs, and my breath came out like smoke. I could see them standing on the corner up ahead. Bliss's arms were wound around Garrick's neck, and the two of them stood wrapped together on the sidewalk. Bundled in coats and scarves, they could have been a magazine ad or one of those perfect pictures that come in the frame when you buy it.

I tried not to be jealous. I was getting over it.

I was.

I wanted Bliss to be happy, and with her hands in Garrick's coat pockets and their breath fogging between them, she definitely looked happy. But that was part of the problem. Even if I managed to let go of my feelings for Bliss completely, it was their happiness that inspired my jealousy.

Because I was fucking miserable. I tried to keep myself busy, made some friends, and settled into life all right here, but it just wasn't the same. Starting over sucked.

On a scale of one to ghetto, my apartment was a solid eight. Things were still awkward with my best friend. I had student loans piling so high I might asphyxiate beneath them at any time. I thought by pursuing my master's degree, I would get at least one part of my life right . . . WRONG.

I was the youngest one in the program, and everyone else had years of working in the real world under his or her belt. The assignments were kicking my ass, and so were the rest of the actors. I'd been here nearly three months, and the only acting I'd done had been a cameo appearance as a homeless person in a Good Samaritan commercial.

Yeah, I was living the good life.

I knew the minute Bliss caught sight of me because she pulled her hands out of Garrick's pockets, and placed them safely at her sides. She stepped out of his arms and called, "Cade!"

I smiled. I guess I was doing some acting after all.

I met them on the sidewalk, and Bliss gave me a hug. Short. Obligatory. Garrick shook my hand. As much as it irked me, I still really liked the guy. He'd never tried to keep Bliss from seeing me, and he'd apparently given me a pretty stellar reference when I applied to Temple. He didn't go around marking his territory or telling me to back off. He smiled and sounded genuine when he said, "It's good to see you, Cade."

"Good to see you guys, too."

There was a moment of awkward silence, and then Bliss gave an exaggerated shiver. "I don't know about you guys, but I'm freezing. Let's head inside."

Together we filed through the door. Mugshots was a coffee place during the day and served alcohol at night. I'd not been there yet as it was kind of a long trek from my apartment up by the Temple campus and because I didn't drink coffee, but I'd heard good things. Bliss loved coffee, and I still loved making Bliss happy, so I agreed to meet there when she called. I thought of asking if they'd serve me alcohol now, even though it wasn't evening yet. Instead, I settled on a smoothie and found us a table big enough that we'd have plenty of personal space.

Bliss sat first, while Garrick waited for their drinks. Her cheeks were pink from the cold, but the winter weather agreed with her. The blue scarf knotted around her neck brought out her eyes, and her curls were scattered across her shoulders, windswept and wonderful.

Damn it. I had to stop doing this.

She pulled off her gloves, and rubbed her hands together. "How are you?" She asked.

I balled my fists under the table and lied, "I'm great. Classes are good. I'm loving Temple. And the city is great. I'm great."

"You are?" I could tell by the look on her face that she knew I was lying. She was my best friend, which made her pretty hard to fool. She'd always been good at reading me . . . except for when it came to how I felt about her. She could pick up on just about all my other fears and insecurities, but never that. Sometimes I wonder if it was wishful thinking. Maybe she didn't pick up on my feelings because she didn't want to.

"I am," I assured her. She still didn't believe me, but she knew me well enough to know that I needed to hold on to my lie. I couldn't vent to her about my problems, not right now. We didn't have that kind of relationship anymore. I wasn't sure we'd ever have that kind of relationship again.

Garrick sat down. He'd brought all three of our drinks. I didn't even hear them call out my order.

"Thanks," I said.

"No problem. What are we talking about?"

Here we go again. I took a long slurp of my smoothie so that I didn't have to answer immediately.

Bliss said, "Cade just finished telling me all about his classes. He's kicking higher education's ass."

Garrick nudged Bliss's drink toward her, and smiled

when she took a long, grateful drink. He turned to me and said, "That's good to hear, Cade. I'm glad it's going well. I'm still on good terms with the professors at Temple, so if you ever need anything, you know you just have to ask."

God, why couldn't he have been an asshole? If he were, one good punch would have gone a long way to easing the tightness in my chest. And it would be much cheaper than punching out a wall in my apartment.

I said, "Thanks. I'll keep that in mind."

We chattered about unimportant things. Bliss talked about their production of *Pride and Prejudice*, and I realized that Garrick really had been good for her. I never would have guessed that out of all of us, she'd be the one doing theatre professionally so quickly after we graduated. It's not that she wasn't talented, but she was never confident. I thought she would have gone the safer route and been a stage manager. I liked to think I could have brought that out of her too, but I wasn't so sure.

She talked about their apartment on the edge of the Gayborhood. So far, I'd managed to wriggle out of all her invitations to visit, but sooner or later I was going to run out of excuses and would have to see the place where they lived. Together.

Apparently, their neighborhood is a pretty big party area. They live right across from a really popular bar. Garrick said, "Bliss is such a light sleeper that it has become a regular event to wake up and listen to the drama that inevitably occurs outside our window at closing time."

She was a light sleeper? I hated that he knew that and I didn't. I hated feeling this way. They started relaying a story of one of those nighttime events, but they were barely looking at me. They stared at each other, laughing, reliving the memory.

I made a promise to myself then that I wouldn't do this again. Not until I had figured all my shit out. This had to be the last time. I smiled and nodded through the rest of the story, and was relieved when Bliss's phone rang.

She looked at the screen, and didn't even explain before she accepted the call and pressed the phone to her ear. "Kelsey? Oh my God! I haven't heard from you in weeks!"

Kelsey had done exactly what she said she would. At the end of the summer, everyone was moving to new cities or new universities, and Kelsey went overseas for the trip of a lifetime. Every time I looked at Facebook, she had added a new country to her list.

Bliss held up a finger, and mouthed "Be right back." She stood and said into the phone, "Kelsey, hold on one sec. I can barely hear you. I'm going to go outside."

I watched her go, remembering when her face used to light up like that talking to me. It was depressing the way life branched off in different directions. I'd spent four years with my college friends, and they felt like family. But now we were scattered across the country and would probably never be all together again.

Garrick said, "Cade, there's something I'd like to talk to you about while Bliss is gone."

This was going to suck. I could tell. Last time we'd had a chat alone, he'd told me that I had to get over Bliss, that I couldn't live my life based on my feelings for her. Damn it if he wasn't still right.

"I'm all ears," I said.

"I don't really know the best way to say—"

"Just say it." That was the worst part of all of this. I'd gotten my heart broken by my best friend, and now everyone tiptoed around me like I was on the verge of meltdown, like a girl with PMS. Apparently having emotions equated to having a vagina.

Garrick took a deep breath. He looked unsure, but in the moments before he spoke, a smile pulled at his face, like he just couldn't help himself.

"I'm proposing to Bliss," He said.

The world went silent, and I heard the tick-tick of the clock on the wall beside us. It sounded like the ticking of a bomb, which was ironic considering all the pieces of me that I had been holding together by sheer force of will had just been blown to bits.

I schooled my features as best as I could, even though I felt like I might suffocate at any moment. I took a beat, which is just a fancy acting word for a pause, but it felt easier if I approached this like a scene, like fiction. Beats are reserved for those moments when something in the scene or your character shifts. They are moments of change.

Man, was this one hell of a beat.

"Cade—"

Before Garrick could say something nice or consoling, I pushed my character, pushed myself back into action. I smiled and made a face that I hoped look congratulatory.

"That's great, man! She couldn't have found a better guy."

It really was just like acting, bad acting anyway. Like when the words didn't feel natural in my mouth and my mind stayed separate from what I was saying no matter how hard

I tried to stay in character. My thoughts raced ahead trying to judge whether or not my audience was buying my performance, whether Garrick was buying it.

"So, you're okay with this?"

It was imperative that I didn't allow myself to pause before I answered, "Of course! Bliss is my best friend, and I've never seen her so happy, which means I couldn't be happier for her."

He reached across the table and patted me on the shoulder, like I was his son or little brother or his dog.

"You're a good man, Cade."

That was me . . . the perpetual good guy, which meant I perpetually came in second. My smoothie tasted bitter on my tongue.

"You had auditions last week, right?" Garrick asked. "How did they turn out?"

Oh please no. I just had to hear about his proposal plans. If I had to follow that up by relaying my complete and utter failure as a grad student, I'd kill myself.

Luckily, I was saved by Bliss's return. She was tucking her phone back into her pocket, and had a wide smile on her face. She stood behind Garrick's chair and placed a hand on his shoulder. I was struck suddenly by the thought that she was going to say yes.

Somewhere deep in my gut, I could feel the certainty of it. And it killed me.

"We have to go, babe," she said to Garrick. "We have call across town in like thirty minutes." She turned to me, "I'm sorry, Cade. I meant for us to have more time to chat, but

Kelsey's been MIA for weeks. I couldn't not answer, and we've got a matinee for a group of students today. I swear I'll make it up to you. Are you going to be able to make it to our Orphan Thanksgiving tomorrow?"

I'd been dodging that invitation for weeks. I was fairly certain that it had been the entire purpose of this coffee meeting. I'd been on the verge of giving in, but now I couldn't. I didn't know when Garrick planned to propose, but I couldn't be around when it happened or after it happened. I needed a break from them, from Bliss, from being the nice guy that never got his way.

"Actually, I forgot to tell you. I'm going to go home for Thanksgiving after all." I hated lying to her, but I just couldn't do it anymore. "Grams hasn't been feeling well, so I thought it was a good idea to go."

Her face pulled into an expression of concern, and her hand reached out toward my arm. I pretended like I didn't see it and stepped away to throw my empty smoothie cup in the trash. "Is she okay?" Bliss asked.

"Oh yeah, I think so. Just a bug probably, but at her age, you never know."

I was definitely on my way to leaving behind my nice-guy persona. I just used my seventy-year-old grandma, the woman who'd raised me, as an excuse. Talk about a douche move.

"Oh, well, tell her I said hi and that I hope she feels better. And you have a safe flight." Bliss leaned in to hug me, and I didn't move away. In fact, I hugged her back. Because I didn't plan on seeing her again for a while, not until I could say (without lying) that I was over her. And based on the way my whole body seemed to sing at her touch, it might take a while.

The two of them packed up to leave, and I sat back down, saying I was going to stay and work on homework for a while. I pulled out a play to read, but in reality, I just wasn't ready for the walk home. I couldn't spend any more alone time locked in my thoughts. The coffee shop was just busy enough that my mind was filled with the buzzing of other people's lives and conversations. Bliss waved through the glass as they left, and I waved back, wondering if she could feel the finality of this good-bye.

2

Max

Mace's hand slid into my back pocket at the same time the phone in my front pocket buzzed. I let him have the three seconds it took for me to grab my phone, then I elbowed him, and he removed his hand.

I'd had to elbow him three times on the way to the coffee shop. He didn't learn that fast.

I looked at the screen, and it showed a picture of my mom that I'd snapped while she wasn't looking. She had been chopping vegetables and looked like a knife-wielding maniac, which she pretty much was, minus the knife.

I jogged the last few steps to Mugshots and slipped inside before answering.

"Hello, Mom."

There was Christmas music on in the background. We hadn't even got Thanksgiving over with, and she was playing Christmas music.

Maniac.

"Hi, sweetie!" She stretched out the end of sweetie so long I thought she was a robot who had just malfunctioned. Then finally she continued, "What are you up to?"

"Nothing, mom. I just popped into Mugshots for a coffee. You remember, it was that place I took you when you and Dad helped me move here."

"I do remember! It was a cute place, pity they serve alcohol."

And there was my mom in a nutshell.

Mace chose that moment (an unfortunately silent moment) to say, "Max, babe, you want your usual?"

I waved him off, and stepped a few feet away.

Mom must have had me on speakerphone because my dad cut in, "And who is that, Mackenzie?"

Mackenzie.

I shuddered. I hated my parents' absolute refusal to call me Max. And if they didn't approve of Max for their baby girl, they sure wouldn't like that I was dating a guy named Mace.

My dad would have an aneurysm.

"Just a guy," I said.

Mace nudged me and rubbed his thumb and fingers together. That's right. He'd been fired from his job. I handed him my purse to pay.

"Is this a guy you're dating?" Mom asked.

I sighed. There wasn't any harm in giving her this, as long as I fudged some of the details. Or, you know, all of them.

"Yes, mom. We've been dating for a few weeks." Try three months, but whatever.

"Is that so? How come we don't know anything about this guy then?" Dad, again.

"Because it's still new. But he's a really nice guy, smart." I don't think Mace actually finished high school, but he was gorgeous and a killer drum player. I wasn't cut out for the type of guy my mother wanted for me. My brain would melt from boredom in a week. That was if I didn't send him running for Mommy before that.

"Where did you meet?" Mom asked.

Oh, you know, he hit on me at the go-go bar where I dance, that extra job that you have no idea I work.

Instead, I said, "The library."

Mace at the library. That was laughable. The tattoo curving across his collarbone would have been spelled "villian" instead of "villain" if I hadn't been there to stop him.

"Really?" Mom sounded skeptical. I didn't blame her. Meeting nice guys at the library wasn't really my thing. Every meet-the-parents thing I'd ever gone through had ended disastrously with my parents certain their daughter had been brainwashed by a godless individual and my boyfriend kicking me to the curb because I had too much baggage.

My baggage was named Betty and Mick and came wearing

polka dots and sweater vests on the way home from bridge club. Sometimes it was hard to believe that I came from them. The first time I died my hair bright pink, my mom burst into tears like I told her I was sixteen and pregnant. God knows what she would do if she saw me today.

It was easier these days just to humor them, especially since they were still helping me out financially so I could spend more time working on my music. And it wasn't that I didn't love them . . . I did. I just didn't love the person they wanted me to be. So, I made small sacrifices. I didn't introduce them to my boyfriends. I died my hair a relatively normal color before any trips home. I took out my piercings and wore long-sleeved, high-neck shirts to cover my tattoos. I told them I worked the front desk at an accounting firm instead of a tattoo parlor, and never mentioned my other job working in a bar.

When I went home, I played at normal for a few days, and then got the hell outta Dodge before my parents could try to set me up with a crusty accountant.

"Yes, Mom. The library."

When I went home for Christmas, I'd just tell her it didn't work out. Or that he was a serial killer. Use that as my excuse to never date nice guys.

"Well, that sounds lovely. We'd love to meet him."

Mace returned to me then with my purse and our coffees. He snuck a flask out of his pocket and added a little something special to his drink. I waved him off when he offered it to me. The caffeine was enough. Funny how he couldn't afford coffee, but he could afford alcohol.

"Sure, Mom." Mace snuck a hand into my coat and

wrapped it around my waist. His hand was large and warm, and his touch through my thin tee made me shiver. "I think you would actually really like him." I finished the sentence on a breathy sigh as Mace's lips found the skin of my neck, and my eyes rolled back in bliss. I'd never met an accountant who could do *that*. "He's very, ah, talented."

"I guess we'll see for ourselves soon," Dad's reply was gruff.

Hah. If they thought there was any chance I was bringing a guy home for Christmas, they were delusional.

"Sure, Dad."

Mace's lips were making a pretty great case for skipping this morning's band practice, but it was our last time to practice all together before our gig next week.

"Great," Dad said, "We'll be at that coffee place in about five minutes."

My coffee hit the floor before I even got a chance to taste it.

"You WHAT? You're not at home in Oklahoma?"

Mace jumped back when the coffee splattered all over our feet. "Max!" I didn't have time to worry about him. I had much bigger issues.

"Don't be mad, honey," Mom said. "We were so sad when you said you couldn't come home for Thanksgiving, then Michael and Bethany decided to visit her family for the holiday, too. So we decided to come visit you. I even special ordered a turkey! Oh, you should invite your new boyfriend. The one from the library."

SHIT. SHIT. ALL OF THE SHITS.

"Sorry, Mom. But I'm pretty sure my boyfriend is busy on Thanksgiving."

Mace said, "No, I'm not." And I don't know if it was all the years of being in a band and the loud music damaging his hearing, or too many lost brain cells, but the guy could just not master a freaking whisper!

"Oh, great! We'll be there in a few minutes, sweetie. Love you, boo boo bear."

If she called me boo boo bear in front of Mace, I wouldn't be responsible for my actions. "Wait, Mom—"

The line went dead.

I kind of wanted to follow its lead.

Think fast, Max. Parentals in T-minus two minutes. Time for damage control.

Mace had maneuvered us around the spilled coffee while I was talking, and he was moving to put his arms back around my waist. I pushed him back.

I took a good look at him—his black, shaggy hair, gorgeous dark eyes, the septum piercing that curved like a bullring from his nostrils, the gauges that stretched his earlobes, and the mechanical skull tattooed on the side of his neck. I loved the way he wore his personality on his skin.

My parents would hate it.

My parents hated anything that couldn't be put organized and labeled and penned safely into a cage. They weren't always that way. They used to listen and judge people on the things that mattered, but that time was long gone, and they'd be here any minute.

"You have to leave," I said.

"What?" He hooked his fingers into my belt loops and tugged me forward until our hips met. "We just got here."

A small part of me thought maybe Mace could handle my

parents. He'd charmed me. He may not have been smart or put together or any of those things, but he was passionate about music and about life. And he was passionate about me. There was fire between us. Fire I didn't want extinguished because my parents were still living in the past, and couldn't get over what had happened to Alex.

"I'm sorry, babe. My parents have made an impromptu visit, and they're going to be here any minute. So, I need you to leave or pretend like you don't know me or something."

I was going to apologize, say that I wasn't ashamed of him, that I just wasn't ready for that. I didn't get a chance before he held his hands up and backed away, "Fuck. No argument here. I'm out." He turned for the door. "Call me when you lose the folks."

Then he bailed. No questions asked. No valiant offer to brave meeting the parents. He walked out the door, lit up a cigarette, and took off. For a second, I thought about following him. Whether to flee or kick his ass, I wasn't sure.

But I couldn't.

Now I just had to figure out what to tell my parents about my suddenly absent library-going-nice-guy-boyfriend. I'd just have to tell them he had to work or go to class or heal the sick or something. I scanned the room for an open table. They'd probably see right through the lie and know there was no nice guy, but there was no way around it.

Damn. The coffee shop was packed, and there weren't any open tables.

There was a four-top with only one guy sitting at it, and it looked like he was almost done. He had short, curly brown hair that had been tamed into something neat and clean. He was gorgeous, in that all-American model kind of way. He wore a sweater and a scarf and had a book sitting on his table. He looked exactly like the kind of guy libraries should use in advertising if they wanted more people to read.

Normally, I wouldn't have looked twice at him because guys like that don't go for girls like me. But he was looking back at me. Staring, actually. He had the same dark, penetrating eyes as Mace, but they were softer somehow. Nicer.

And it was like the universe was giving me a gift. All that was missing was a flashing neon sign above his head that said, "Answer to all your problems."